ANOTHER CHANCE

School teacher Rowan Fairlie's life is set to change when Clett Drummond and his two young daughters take on the tenancy of Ballinbrae Farm. Clett insists he's come to the Highlands to help the girls recover from their mother's death, but Rowan suspects there's more to it. And why does her growing friendship with the family so infuriate the new laird, Simon Fraser? Is it simple jealousy — or are the two men linked by some terrible mystery from the past?

Books by Rena George
in the Linford Romance Library:

DANGER AT MELLIN COVE

RENA GEORGE

ANOTHER CHANCE

Complete and Unabridged

LINFORD
Leicester

First published in Great Britain in 2012

First Linford Edition
published 2013

A catalogue record for this book is available
from the British Library.

ISBN 978–1–4448–1646–4

Published by
F. A. Thorpe (Publishing)
Anstey, Leicestershire

Set by Words & Graphics Ltd.
Anstey, Leicestershire
Printed and bound in Great Britain by
T. J. International Ltd., Padstow, Cornwall

This book is printed on acid-free paper

Highland Home

It was early, but there was no shortage of activity around the tiny harbour. The days of the commercial fishing boats might be long gone, but Balcreggan men would always sail out of this loch, just as their grandfathers had done, and their grandfathers before them. And if they caught a few crabs or the occasional lobster to sell on to a local hotel then that was a bonus.

Rowan Fairlie stood in front of the neat white-washed cottage where she'd grown up and watched the boats mirrored in the harbour water.

Sounds of a chugging engine, the grating of a rusty winch chain and the voices of the men as they joked with each other drifted to her from across the quay. Life was lived to a very different beat here in this corner of the Scotland.

She took a deep breath, enjoying the sensation of the pure Highland air filling her lungs and reminded herself for the umpteenth time just how lucky she was to be home.

A voice made her start.

'Just the girl I was hoping to meet.' Simon Fraser's grey eyes were smiling this morning. 'I have a treat for you, Rowan.'

He flapped two gold embossed tickets in her face.

'We're going to the Highland Ball next weekend!'

He waited for her excited reaction, but that didn't happen.

'I'm sorry, Simon. I can't come — I have a previous arrangement.'

'What do you mean, you can't come?'

She saw the muscles in his jaw flex, as they always did when things were not going his way, but her decision had been made and she would not be swayed.

Not even if half the population of

Balcreggan appeared to be eavesdropping, as they were, on their conversation at the moment.

She wasn't one of his tenant farmers, nor an estate worker, or beholden to him in any other way. They were supposed to be friends, and in Rowan's book that meant considering each other's point of view.

He threw an irritated glance back to the harbour and frowned at the two boat owners who had been following the little scene with some amusement.

He lowered his voice and the words came out in an angry hiss.

'We shouldn't be discussing this here.' He nodded towards the pub. 'Let's have a drink and discuss this in a civilised way.'

Rowan sighed and tapped her watch.

'Not open yet. Besides, I'm expected somewhere else and I'm already late. Sorry, Simon.'

His eyebrows met in a confused frown and he glanced to the low cottage behind her.

'I assumed, when your car was parked here, that you were calling on your mother.'

'Yes, and I'm already late.'

'Evelyn won't mind if we go for a coffee!'

'Look, Simon, I've already told you I don't want to go with you to the Highland Ball.'

She shook her head and her shining cap of dark hair swung out and back into place.

'I'm not going to change my mind, no matter how many cups of coffee you ply me with.'

She saw the colour rising in his handsome face and wondered if she'd gone too far.

The ball was the social event of the year in the Highlands. It was the opportunity for wealthy businessmen such as Simon to mingle with Scotland's elite.

Rowan was an ordinary primary school teacher and would feel like a fish out of water in such company.

Simon's eyes had narrowed.

'Have you any idea how many strings I had to pull to get these tickets? And it wasn't easy getting two rooms in the Inverlochy Hotel.' He emphasised the word 'two'. 'All the decent Inverness hotels are booked up months in advance for an occasion like this.'

His voice was rising again and Rowan could see a pair of village women glancing back as they passed. Their heads were together, enjoying the pleasure they would have relating this little incident to all who would listen.

'Well, I'm sorry.' Rowan's shoulders rose in a shrug. 'But you didn't consult me before making arrangements on my behalf.'

Balcreggan Primary was just a tiny village school, and apart from Helen Gemmel, a part-time teaching assistant, Rowan was its only fully qualified teacher.

She had responsibilities, and weekends were spent planning projects that the children would enjoy in the coming week.

'Can't you find someone else to take?'

Simon stared at her as though she were mad.

'Of course I can't. It's you I want with me, Rowan.' He looked away, exasperated. 'But if it's more important to you to stay here, playing headmistress, rather than supporting me then there's no more to be said.'

Before she had a chance to respond he had turned on his heel and was striding across to the shiny, green four-by-four he'd parked by the harbour.

He jumped in, rammed it into gear and took off in a cloud of dust through the village.

Rowan stared furiously after him. The man's arrogance was appalling. Of course her job was more important to her than being paraded on Simon Fraser's arm as some kind of trophy girlfriend. Even if he did now own Balcreggan Estate and most of the cottages in the village.

'Is this a bad time?' A deep male voice cut across her thoughts.

Rowan looked up, still seething at Simon's petulance.

A man was sitting at the wheel of a mud-encrusted Jeep across the road.

'You are Miss Fairlie, aren't you?' he called. The accent wasn't local and Rowan was struggling to place it.

'I'm sorry. Did you want to speak to me?'

He climbed out of his vehicle and walked with a slow, confident stride towards her.

'Clett Drummond.' He extended his hand and nodded in the direction of the fields that sloped away from the far side of the harbour. 'I'm the new tenant at Ballinbrae Farm.'

They shook hands.

'You're very young to be a head teacher, if you don't mind my saying so.'

Rowan could feel her colour rising under his stare.

7

'That's a bit of a misnomer, I'm afraid. Balcreggan Primary is a tiny school and we don't have enough pupils to justify more than one class.' She shrugged. 'So it's just me and my class assistant.'

He smiled, but it didn't reach his eyes, as green as the sparkling waters of the loch. A shadow of sadness in those eyes made Rowan want to reach out and touch him.

So this was the Clett Drummond that had got the village talking! It was obvious why his arrival had set female hearts fluttering, and from his manner she guessed that he would be more than able to deal with Simon.

The whole village had heard about the Drummond family's tragic history. Just over a year ago Mrs Drummond had been killed in a car crash, leaving him to bring up their two young daughters on his own.

No wonder the man looked sad.

She realised he was still watching her and she raised an eyebrow, but she knew what he was here to say.

'My girls,' he said. 'I need to enrol them in school.'

'How old are they?'

'Charlotte's nine and Poppy's seven.'

'That's fine. Bring them along on Monday morning at around nine-thirty.' That would get the class settled before Rowan could leave them with Helen.

Clett Drummond nodded.

'We'll see you then.'

He turned and walked back to his farm Jeep without the trace of a smile, though he did lift his hand in a casual wave as he drove off.

Rowan was thoughtful as she turned towards the little white cottage.

Evelyn Fairlie was checking the progress of a chicken casserole in the oven, but her face, still flushed from the heat, broke into a smile when she saw her daughter coming through the back door.

'This is almost ready. Come away in, Rowan, and take your coat off and sit down.'

She pulled out a kitchen chair, taking a quick glance at her daughter's face.

'Nothing wrong, is there?'

Rowan smiled as she hung her jacket on the hook beside the back door. She'd told Simon her mother had been expecting her, but it had been a white lie.

'Do I need an excuse to visit my mother?'

'Of course not. You know I'm always pleased to see you. In fact, why don't you stay for a bit of lunch? This will be ready in no time and there's plenty for two.'

There was a salmon steak sitting in Rowan's fridge up at the schoolhouse, but the thought of eating alone suddenly didn't appeal, and the delicious smell of the casserole filling the kitchen swept aside any resistance.

'Thanks, Mum.'

Evelyn sat down and studied her daughter.

'Have you had a falling out with somebody? Is that what's wrong? Some

10

of those parents have too much to say
for themselves.'

Rowan shook her head, laughing.

'I told you, Mum. There's nothing
wrong. I'm just a bit tired, that's all.'

She wasn't in a mood for repeating
the exchange she'd so recently had with
Simon. But her mother's ability to see
through her was infuriating.

Rowan sighed and ran a hand
through her short hair, pushing straying
dark locks behind her ear.

'I met Simon down at the harbour
and he invited me to the Highland
Ball.'

'And why would that upset you?'
Evelyn was staring at her daughter with
a quizzical frown. 'Don't tell me you
refused!'

'Of course I did. He knows how busy
I am at weekends, planning the class
projects for the coming week. Besides,
he didn't ask first if I even wanted to
go. He just made an assumption and
bought the tickets.'

She looked up at her mother from

under dark lashes.

'He booked rooms, as well, in the Inverlochy Hotel — before he'd even checked with me!'

Evelyn rolled her eyes.

'I don't know what you're thinking of, Rowan. Every other lass in the village would give her right arm to go out with Simon Fraser, never mind be taken to the fancy Highland Ball. Why, he's practically the Laird.'

'Simon's not the Laird!' Rowan protested. 'Not to me. Sir Alex was the Laird, and now he's gone.'

'And now we have Simon Fraser — very much alive.'

Her mother was right. Simon was eligible enough, but he was unpredictable, and she couldn't make herself have feelings for him.

It wasn't that she didn't enjoy his company, but theirs was a friendship, not a romance, though she suspected that Simon was no longer satisfied with that.

His outburst earlier was out of

frustration and she knew he would now be regretting it. But the words had been said, and Rowan suspected there was more than a grain of truth in them. Simon was not really supportive of her teaching career, but she had no intention of giving it up. Not for him, or for anyone else!

'I met the new tenant farmer at Ballinbrae,' she said to her mother to stem any further comments. 'He's coming to enrol his two daughters in school on Monday.'

Evelyn's expression took on a look of compassion.

'That little family has had a bad time of things this past year, what with his poor wife having died so young and him left to bring up two wee lassies on his own. It's not every man who could cope with such a thing.'

Her voice fell.

'Bad enough when it happens to a woman.'

Evelyn looked away, but not before Rowan saw her blink back a tear.

Hugh Fairlie had died after a heart attack five years ago.

★　★　★

When Rowan had got the appointment at the tiny Balcreggan Primary — where she herself had been taught as a child — she'd been delighted at the chance to return to the village where she'd grown up.

She loved the idea of being back with her family. From her kitchen window in the schoolhouse she could see the chimneys of Craigie House where her older sister, Shona, lived with husband, Rory, Hannah, who was eight, and six-year-old Josh.

It had been a shock when Sir Alexander Gifford-Bane died. He had never married, and the estate had been put on the market.

Rowan imagined his successors would bring an army of staff and estate workers with them. Sir Alex had coped with the task almost single-handedly since her father had died. Hugh Fairlie had been estate manager at Balcreggan for twenty years.

The huge sprawling estate, with its farm steadings, woods and pastures, stream and pond, had been the young Rowan's playground. Whenever she got the chance she would accompany her father in his various duties, overseeing the farms, checking on fences, caring for the trees. Not even the Big House was out of bounds.

Everyone had loved Sir Alex. She could see him now, his big wiry frame in a tweed jacket with huge leather patches at the elbows, as he strode through the village with a purposeful gait. He knew everyone by name and stopped to chat, doffing his cap to the ladies. His two dogs, Clyde and Tay, were always by his side, as old and gentle as their master.

His death almost a year ago had saddened the whole community. Rowan returned home from Glasgow where she was teaching to attend the funeral.

Sitting next to her mother and sister at the back of the packed church she blinked back tears as, one by one, villagers stepped up to recount their memories of the man.

Every now and again Rowan caught sight of a woman in black at the front, her back ramrod straight. The handsome sandy-haired man sitting next to her took occasional glances over his shoulder, as though surprised at the size of the turnout for the old Laird's funeral.

Evelyn followed her daughter's gaze.

'That's the new owner of Balcreggan Estate, Simon Fraser,' she whispered. 'He's been more or less running things on the estate since he arrived.'

Her glance shifted to the rigid shoulders of the woman next to him.

'And that's his mother, Mrs Geraldine Fraser. I hope she's not going to be as snooty as she looks!'

Rowan gave her mother a sharp nudge and frowned, lifting an eyebrow in warning to say no more. Evelyn

Fairlie was not known in Balcreggan for holding her tongue when she had something to say. But this was not the time or the place.

The Frasers put in a brief appearance at the wake, which was held down by the harbour at the Crab and Creel, the pub where Sir Alex had enjoyed a daily pint.

But Rowan had hardly noticed them. Her attention was so taken up meeting and greeting old friends that she seldom even looked in the direction of Simon Fraser and his mother.

It was then that Rowan discovered the teaching post at the local primary was soon to become available. Miss Martin, who had been in sole charge of the school for as long as Rowan could remember, came up behind her.

'Has your mother told you I'm retiring at the end of next month?' Her kindly blue eyes crinkled in the same caring way Rowan remembered. 'Why don't you apply for the job, my dear? I think you would be perfect.'

'Yes, why not, Rowan?' Evelyn had come up behind them, and Rowan sensed a conspiracy going on.

Yet it was something to think about. So she applied holding out little hope of actually getting it, since she did not have all the qualifications the board was looking for.

To her delight, she was offered an interview. And when she was finally offered the job she had no hesitation in accepting it.

As a local girl returning to the village where she was brought up, the community expected her to support local activities, but this was no hardship.

The first thing was a Bring and Buy Sale. She had offered to help her mum and Dolly Meikle, a former classmate who was now the school cook, to organise it at the church hall.

It was the day she'd officially met Simon Fraser. Geraldine Fraser had graciously agreed to open the event, but things became a bit of a shamble. Balcreggan women, and those from the surrounding villages, were ruthless in their search for bargains. Garments were snatched up, examined, and discarded again as the shoppers searched for just the right thing.

In the warm hall the atmosphere soon became hot and sticky and Mrs Fraser peeled off her smart grey coat and laid it carefully over a chair.

Some minutes later her voice rang out.

'Where's my coat? I left it here and now it's gone!'

The pink flush on Dolly's face deepened.

'What did it look like?'

Upon hearing a description of the coat, Rowan's eyes flew open as she stared at her friend.

In answer to the unspoken question, Dolly nodded.

'I think I sold it!'

There had been no option but to come clean and admit the catastrophe. Amid profuse apologies, Rowan and Dolly assured the woman they would retrieve her coat and return it good as new.

'One good thing,' Evelyn said, later, making no effort to disguise her amusement at the day's events. 'I think we got a good price for the precious coat.'

It took them two days to track down the buyer and return Mrs Fraser's coat. Rowan was feeling pleased with herself as she stood before the double oak doors of Balcreggan House ringing the shiny brass bell, with the grey coat draped across her arm. She followed a maid into the big bright sitting-room.

She had to blink to make sure it was the same room she had remembered. In Sir Alex's day it had been oak-panelled, and the rugs on which Clyde and Tay slept were threadbare.

That had all gone. Ivory walls were hung with modern paintings — a bit too garish for Rowan's taste — and Sir Alex's battered, old, red leather arm-chairs had been replaced with elegant cream sofas.

Simon Fraser and his mother sat opposite each other, each reading a newspaper.

'Your coat, Mrs Fraser.' Rowan smiled. 'I don't think it's come to any harm.'

Geraldine Fraser lowered her spectacles.

'My coat?'

Rowan held it out.

'That old thing. You don't imagine that I would wear it now, do you, dear?' She gave the garment a disparaging look. 'Keep it for your next jumble sale.'

She softened her reaction with a condescending smile.

'Call it my donation.'

Rowan's face fell.

Simon, who had sprung to his feet when she came into the room, now strode towards Rowan.

'Mother! Where are your manners? This lady has gone to a great deal of trouble to retrieve your coat, and this is how you thank her!'

Rowan coloured. She was getting annoyed now.

'It's perfectly all right. I'm sure someone will appreciate it.' She turned on her heel and marched out of the room with Simon in hot pursuit.

'I don't even know your name!'

She stopped and turned back.

'I'm Rowan Fairlie. I'm the teacher at Balcreggan Primary School.'

At least she knew how to behave, even if other people didn't!

He smiled down at her, extending his hand as he did so.

'I'm Simon Fraser. I really am sorry about my mother. She can be a bit sharp sometimes. She doesn't mean any harm. Let me make amends. May I buy you dinner this evening, Miss Fairlie?'

She hadn't intended to accept, but it didn't make sense falling out with these people, which was why later that evening she found herself seated opposite him in the rather formal surroundings of the dining room at the St Leonard's Hotel, in the nearby town of Invermore.

It was mid-week and only three other

tables were occupied. Simon looked around the room and grimaced, then ran a finger along the inside of his collar in a gesture of discomfort.

'I should have taken you somewhere else.'

Rowan followed his stare.

'It's not that bad,' she said. 'And I've heard the food is very good.'

He looked at her and they both burst out laughing. He stood up, grabbing her hand.

'I'm sure it is, but let's find out another time!'

In the street outside he turned to face her.

'Any ideas where we could go?'

Rowan pursed her lips while she considered.

'There's the Clunie Inn. It's not as posh as this place, but they don't stand on ceremony and the food is great.'

'What are we waiting for? Lead the way!'

★   ★   ★

23

'You were right about the food.' He touched the crimson napkin to his lips. 'That was one of the best steak pies I have ever tasted.'

He glanced down at Rowan's plate, which held the remnants of the lemon sole and delicate parsley sauce she'd chosen from the menu.

'How was yours?'

Rowan laid down her knife and fork and swallowed her last mouthful.

'Delicious.'

They declined the array of sweet deserts on a trolley, choosing instead to have biscuits and an assortment of cheeses. Rowan watched him sip the robust red wine he'd ordered for them both.

'What made you buy Balcreggan Estate, Mr Fraser?'

'I thought you were to call me Simon?'

She gave him an embarrassed smile.

'But to answer your question, I bought Balcreggan because . . . well, because I could!'

Rowan was shocked. She didn't like the sound of that at all.

'That's no reason,' she said, sharply. 'The estate comes with so many responsibilities. The livelihoods of almost half the people in the village depend on you!'

She could never have imagined Sir Alex ever saying anything so ridiculous and wondered if he would even have sold the place to someone with that philosophy. But then he hadn't had a say in it.

Simon's eyes twinkled and he held up his hands as though to fend off any further rebuke.

'I was joking, you know. You musn't take me so seriously.'

'I don't see it as a joke to be in charge of such an important place.'

'Sorry. I shouldn't have treated your question so lightly. The fact is that I have always wanted to own a place like this.'

He looked up and smiled at her.

'And before you ask, the answer is

no, I have no background in this kind of business. I buy and sell properties. I buy when they are rundown, make improvements, and then resell at a profit.'

He shrugged.

'That's my business, and I'm good at it. I run a company based in Inverness called Highland Properties.'

'You buy and sell! Does that mean you don't intend to keep Balcreggan Estate?' Alarm bells were ringing.

'On the contrary, I plan to settle here. That's why I've brought my mother to stay. This kind of life suits us both.'

Criminal Damage

That had been almost a year ago. Over the months, Mrs Fraser's high-handed attitude to the local community had earned her few friends. And Rowan was beginning to realise that her son was not averse to confrontation, either.

Simon had a way of upsetting people. He was considerate to her and generous in his donations to the school, but in Balcreggan he was not popular. So it was no surprise when, a couple of days after her quarrel with Simon, there was an urgent hammering on the school-house door.

'Have you seen it?' Dolly rushed past Rowan into her warm kitchen. 'Have you seen what he's done now?'

Rowan sighed. What now? Dolly's round face was bright with indignation as she made a beeline for the window, pushed aside a bowl of fat blue hyacinths and strained for a glimpse of the harbour.

'Look,' she insisted, grabbing Rowan's hand. 'You can just about see it from here. No, not there . . . look!' She pushed Rowan to where she could have a better view.

'Look at what?' Rowan peered over the cottage roofs.

'Your young laird has only put up a gate, that's all! He has no right! The men will have that down before the end of the day, you'll see.'

Rowan was still mystified about what had caused Dolly's agitation. Then she spotted it; a new cross-barred gate right across the entrance to the waterside walk.

This was a well-trodden track which led from the harbour along to the end of the peninsula, and a popular Sunday walk. Flat along the shoreline, it banked steeply to the right and up to what were now Clett Drummond's fields. Ballinbrae farmhouse was set further up the hill on the country road that eventually passed the village school.

On summer evenings, when the water lapped gently on to the pebbled shore, it was a peaceful retreat. Rowan knew that, if Balcreggan folk had no legal right to use it, they certainly had a moral one.

And Simon was out of order by denying it to them.

Dolly was talking again.

'That nice Mr Drummond won't be able to get his tractor down there now, because it's impossible to reach that bottom field from the top.' She slid a glance to Rowan. 'He's not going to appreciate that.'

Dolly was right. Clett Drummond might have his difficulties at the moment but he didn't strike Rowan as the sort of man who would tolerate this kind of thing.

'Honestly, Rowan, I don't know what you see in that Simon.' Dolly let out an exasperated sigh.

Rowan flashed her friend a mischievous grin.

'You mean apart from him being a rich landowner and the most eligible bachelor this side of Inverness?'

Dolly's round grey eyes widened.

'Rowan Fairlie! I'm surprised at you. You'll be telling us next that you want to be the next lady of the manor.'

'If I had ambitions in that direction — which I don't — I think his mother would have something to say about it.'

'He's a dangerous man that one, Rowan. You should watch your step with him.'

The toaster flipped out the two slices of bread she had put in when Dolly burst into the kitchen and she turned to butter them while they were still hot.

She was smiling, but Rowan knew her friend was right. She hadn't intended getting into a relationship with Simon Fraser. Their frequent dinner dates had been bound to set tongues wagging but she didn't like his cavalier attitude to things any more than the rest of the community did.

In the beginning it had seemed like a

good idea for the primary school teacher to be on good terms with the local estate owner. His support for school projects had been invaluable. But things were starting to get out of hand. She was remembering the recent embarrassing scene at the harbour.

It was obvious that Simon wanted more from their relationship. He'd even hinted at marriage. Rowan wasn't ready for that — certainly not with Simon. Maybe the time had come to tell him so.

Dolly's voice startled her.

'So what are you going to do about it?'

'Do?'

'The gate!' She jabbed a finger towards the window. 'What are you going to do about it?'

Rowan sighed.

'I'm not sure it's my business to get involved.'

'Well, if you don't, the villagers will take things into their own hands. They'll have that gate down in no time.'

'We can't let them do that.'

Rowan was trying to keep her voice calm. Simon was a powerful man in the community. Many families depended on the jobs he provided. She didn't doubt he would have his revenge if the villagers damaged estate property.

To stand by while they tore out his gate was unthinkable, even if she did understand their anger.

'You'll have to talk to Fraser, Rowan. You're the only one he'll listen to.'

Rowan's shoulders rose in resignation. Dolly was right.

'I'll go over and talk to him today.' She raised a finger. 'I'm not promising anything, mind. I'm saying I'll try.'

Dolly's face cracked into the kind of smile that knocked ten years off her.

'That's all I'm asking.' Her mobile phone trilled and she fished it out of her pocket. 'Sam?'

Rowan saw a flicker of fear in Dolly's eyes.

'Don't you get involved, Sam Meikle. This isn't your fight.' She listened for a second. 'I don't care about that. You're not to get involved, Sam. Do you hear me?'

Rowan's own eyes were now wide with concern.

'What's happened, Dolly?'

'That trouble we were talking about, Rowan. It's just gone up a notch. You'd better come with me.'

Rowan grabbed Dolly's arm as she went for the door.

'Not before you tell me what's going on.'

Dolly turned to face her, her eyes blazing.

'It's that damned gate, that's what! Sam says the whole village is down there at the harbour. They're threatening to yank it off its hinges.'

'What are we waiting for?' She reached for her jacket on its peg behind the kitchen door.

★ ★ ★

Rowan counted more than a dozen Balcreggan men milling around the gate which, Rowan noted thankfully, seemed still to be in one piece. Not as many as she'd feared, but it wasn't long before she realised that others were joining the crowd and fervour was rising.

Rowan saw Sam Meikle's ginger head at the front of the group. He turned at Dolly's shout and joined them.

'Well, at least there's no damage done.' Rowan breathed a sigh of relief.

'Not yet, there isn't, but that's because they're waiting for Clett Drummond.'

'What do you mean, Sam?' she asked, her fears rising again.

'He's gone back to the farm to get some tools. He's going to tear this thing down!' He shot his wife a defiant glance before his eyes swept over the crowd. 'And he won't be short of helpers.'

Rowan left them at a run. She knew if she ran up Brae Hill and cut out across the fields she could reach

Ballinbrae Farm quicker than any vehicle. Hadn't she done it often enough as a girl?

With its commanding view of the peninsula, the farm was surrounded on three sides by water. The area was spectacularly beautiful, especially in spring when the hedgerows were splurges of wild broom the colour of golden cornfields. The musky scent could still make her feel nostalgic for the days when she ran through these same fields with the other village children.

She was breathless when she reached the farmhouse, just in time to see Clett tossing an armful of tools into the back of his Jeep. He was about to get behind the wheel when he spotted her.

'Miss Fairlie! There's not a problem about the girls starting school on Monday, is there?'

She was puffing to get her breath back.

'I haven't come about them, Mr Drummond.' She pointed to the tools.

'I hope these aren't intended for the purpose I think they are?'

His eyebrow arched in surprise and she thought she caught a glint of amusement in the green eyes.

'And why would that be, Miss Fairlie? Has something happened?'

'Not yet. But if you carry out this threat to pull down Simon Fraser's new gate then I suspect all hell might break loose.'

He stared at her from under lowered brows, a frown creasing the space between the emerald eyes that no longer looked amused.

'You look as though you need a drink. Come inside.'

It was more of a command than an invitation. Rowan suspected that Clett Drummond was used to people doing what they were told, so she followed him into the big rambling farmhouse kitchen. It wasn't exactly unfamiliar to her; she'd been here with her father many times before. It had always been a special treat, when he made his calls on the estate's tenants.

She glanced about her. There was no sign of the children, and Annie Moncrief, the cheery village woman Clett Drummond had employed as his housekeeper, didn't seem to be around either.

He went to a cupboard and took out a glass, which he filled with water from the tap.

'Drink this. It will make you feel better.'

Rowan took a quick gulp. The cold water slid down her throat, its icy purity reaching every part of her.

'Did you come across the fields?' There was no friendly glint in his intense stare. 'Well, what is it? Is there a fire? Has war broken out?'

'That could be closer to the truth than you realise, Mr Drummond. It's that gate.' She blurted out the words with more drama than she had intended. 'You can't pull it down. It would be criminal damage.'

Clett let out a sigh and rolled his eyes.

'So that's why you're here. Fraser's sent you. Can he not do his own dirty work? Does he need to hide behind his . . . ' He paused. 'Well, what are you? His girlfriend, I suppose.'

Rowan jumped to her feet, her blue eyes blazing.

'Simon Fraser did not send me, and I am most certainly not his girlfriend. I just don't want to see anyone getting hurt. Those people are my friends, Mr Drummond, and you are about to involve them in a criminal act.'

Even though she was standing he still towered above her.

'I fight my own battles.' He glared. 'I don't need anybody else's help to do what's necessary. Fraser knows I can't farm this land without access to the bottom fields. I'm merely removing an unnecessary obstruction.'

'You're taking the law into your own hands. What happened to negotiation?'

'Fraser didn't do much negotiating before he put the gate up.' He frowned. 'He doesn't like people talking back to him, either, does he?'

Rowan wasn't giving up just yet.

'Mr Drummond,' she said, determined not to flinch under his gaze, 'I understand that you're angry, but you have your family to consider — your girls. If you pull that gate down then this whole thing will escalate and the police will become involved. I don't know the details of your tenancy contract, but it seems to me you might give Mr Fraser cause to end it.'

Clett said nothing, but his brow was furrowed as though he was considering what she'd said.

She leaned forward.

'Why did he erect the gate, anyway?'

'We don't get on,' he said briefly, examining the long, tanned fingers that didn't look like any farmer's hand Rowan had ever seen. 'I wanted to buy the farm, but Fraser didn't want to split up the estate. His agent in Inverness offered me the lease, and I accepted.' He paused. 'Fraser and I hadn't met at that point, and by the time we did I think he regretted the arrangement. But the papers had been signed.'

'But that's just it! The papers were signed and you have a contract. It binds Simon Fraser as much as you. And I suspect that it's you who has the law on your side.'

Clett was now looking as though he was actually listening to her. She pressed on.

'If this gate has barred access to land you need to work, then it's Simon Fraser who must see reason. Let me talk to him.'

He met her gaze, and although the pale eyes were not exactly smiling, they seemed a little less stern.

'OK, though I'm used to doing my own talking.' He glanced up at the clock. 'I have to collect my daughters from the train, so if you'll excuse me . . . '

'Of course.'

'They've been shopping in Inverness with my housekeeper, Mrs Moncrief,' he added.

Annie Moncrief had run the late Sir Alex's household. Some village gossips had suggested their relationship was more than just employer and employee, but there was no doubting her devotion to the old man.

Simon had apparently assumed she would continue working for him, but Annie had had different ideas and left her employment soon after Simon and his mother moved into Balcreggan House.

'You'll leave the gate in place until I talk to Simon?'

'Fraser has until six o'clock tonight. I'm promising nothing after that.'

As Clett drove to the railway station, Rowan made her way back to the harbour. Time had taken the anger out of the situation, and when she arrived it was clear that some men had already left while others were drifting towards the pub, just opening. She joined Dolly and Sam, who were also heading in the direction of the pub and shared what had happened.

'So there's to be a truce. How long will that last, I wonder,' Dolly said.

'I hope until it's resolved. I'll talk to Simon.'

'Good luck with that, Rowan,' Sam said. 'I've a suspicion you might need it.'

How Dare He?

Two hours later, the tyres of Rowan's bright yellow Mini crunched noisily over the gravelled drive. The house was large and square, with high stone pillars flanking impressive old oak doors. Rowan knocked and one of the heavy doors swung open to reveal a slight, ginger-haired woman in a black and white maid's uniform.

'Hello, Maisie.' Rowan smiled. 'Is Mr Fraser in?'

'He's not home.' Maisie Gillespie wasn't known for her friendliness. 'I'll see if Mrs Fraser is available.'

Before Rowan had a chance to stop her she had turned on her heel and marched off. Rowan sighed. The last person she wanted to see today was Simon's mother. No doubt he'd told her of Rowan's refusal to accompany him to the social event of the year.

She heard the click of the older woman's heels.

'Rowan, dear. What will you think of us? How stupid of Gillespie to leave you standing at the door. Do come inside.'

Indicating towards one of the big cream sofas she invited her guest to sit.

'I'm afraid Simon is out on the estate. Some problem with one of the tenant farmers, I believe. He'll be back within the hour.'

Rowan gave her brightest smile.

'It's not important. Simon wasn't expecting me, or anything.' She stood up. 'I can catch up with him later.'

Geraldine Fraser opened her mouth to speak, but Rowan was already on her way to the door. As she turned to thank her hostess she thought she caught a glimpse of disappointment in the woman's calculating blue eyes.

She'd reached her car when Simon's car roared up, scattering sprays of gravel as it came to a sudden stop.

'Rowan! Are you looking for me?'

'Yes, but if you're busy it can wait.'

'I'm never too busy to see you. What is it?'

He left her with no option.

'It's that gate, Simon. It's causing so much trouble in the village.'

She saw him frown.

'Has Drummond put you up to this? I saw you two talking as I drove off yesterday.'

'Clett Drummond? No, I'm talking about how the people of Balcreggan feel. Unless you want a full-scale riot on your hands you must remove that gate.'

He folded his arms.

'And just why would I want to do that?'

'Because it means a lot to people. It's a special place down there, where folks go when they need to think.'

The memories were flooding back. She could see herself sitting on the bank with her father in his old tweed jacket as he kept an eye on a fishing line in the water. She was on her tummy gazing, enchanted, at the tiny dark minnows darting amongst the weeds.

Simon's voice cut across her thoughts.

'This would have nothing to do with Drummond's tractor, then?'

'What?'

Simon glanced around him.

'Look, we can't discuss this here. Why don't you come for dinner tonight? We can talk the whole thing out then.'

Rowan frowned. Was he was up to something? But talking the whole thing out in a calm, reasonable way was not a bad idea.

It would let her explain how important that waterside walk was to everyone. To convince him that he must remove the offending gate. She nodded.

'If you really are prepared to listen, then I'll come.'

★   ★   ★

A vehicle raced towards her as she left Balcreggan House. The driver sped past without a sideways glance in her direction, but it was a face she

46

recognised. Rowan glanced in the mirror in time to see the muddy Jeep turn in at the gates at great speed.

She grinned. Simon wouldn't get round Clett Drummond with dinner!

As she arrived at Balcreggan that evening, the front door opened even before she reached it. Simon came forward, arms outstretched to greet her.

'You look beautiful,' he murmured, brushing his lips against her cheek. She'd chosen a short-sleeved cream dress in soft wool and was glad to see Simon was in a casual cord jacket and light trousers. At least they weren't dressing for dinner.

Geraldine waited to greet them in her elegant drawing-room. The sherry glass by her side was empty and she waved it at Simon for a refill.

'Rowan, dear. Come and sit by me.' She patted the space beside her on the sofa.

Rowan did as she was told and accepted the glass of sherry Simon handed to her. She would have preferred mineral water. It was so like him not to give her a choice.

No mention was made of the gate all through dinner, and Rowan realised that if the subject was to be broached then it would be up to her. They had moved back into the drawing-room for coffee. As she stirred her cup with a tiny silver spoon, Rowan gave her brightest smile.

'Have you given any more thought to that gate business, Simon?'

He got up and strode across to the window. The curtains had not yet been drawn and she could see his reflection in the dark glass. His expression was stern but in the next second, when he spun round to face her, he was smiling.

'Persuade me,' he invited.

He obviously had no intention of mentioning his tenant farmer's visit. Rowan placed the delicate china cup and saucer carefully on the nearby table.

'I thought I said everything this afternoon. It's cruel to deny the villagers access to their waterside. I told you how important that walk is to all of us.'

'Rowan, I'm sure Simon knows what he is doing,' Geraldine broke in. 'It is private land, after all. The villagers should realise that they have had a privilege all these years, and be grateful for that.'

'Sir Alex never minded us using the place,' Rowan spat back. 'In fact, he often used to walk there himself.'

'Well, Simon is running the estate now, and the decision is his!' Her voice rose.

Simon cleared his throat and raised an eyebrow at his mother. She stood up.

'I'm sure you two young people have much to talk about, so if you will excuse me . . . ' She bestowed a dazzling smile on Rowan. 'It's been lovely having your company tonight, my dear. I do hope we can do this again.'

Once his mother had left, Simon filled two brandy glasses and handed one to Rowan.

'You shouldn't pay too much attention to Mother. She enjoys playing Dowager Duchess. She thinks I can do no wrong.'

'We all do wrong sometimes.'

'I take it we're still talking about that blessed gate.' He pursed his lips. 'What if I told you I would remove it?'

'Is there a catch?'

He gave her a teasing smile.

'Maybe a tiny one.'

'Ah.' She nodded.

'You really would enjoy coming with me to that ball next weekend, you know, Rowan.' He moved closer.

Rowan's mouth dropped open. How dare he use this as a bargaining tool to persuade her to accompany him to the posh dance? Her eyes blazed.

Simon put up a hand.

'Oh, I know I haven't apologised yet for my behaviour yesterday. I shouldn't have taken it for granted that you would want to go to the Highland Ball with me. I know you take your job seriously.'

Rowan shook her head, her eyes wide

with disbelief at his deviousness. She didn't trust herself to say another word. She got up and strode angrily from the room.

She didn't drive directly to the schoolhouse but instead turned down to the harbour. The place was quiet at this time of night. Those who were going to the pub were already in there.

She parked and walked to Simon's gate. But it wasn't there! She stared disbelievingly at the spot where it had been. There was no sign of it ever having been there.

Sunday Lunch

'I see that gate's been taken down,' Evelyn said as Rowan walked into her bright, sunny kitchen next morning. 'I don't know what you said to that young man of yours, but it certainly did the trick.'

'Simon Fraser is not my young man, Mum. How many times do I have to tell you?' She was struggling to bite back her annoyance. 'I hope you haven't been spreading that rumour in the village.'

Her mother looked fondly at her daughter.

'People have eyes, Rowan. They know you and Simon have been seeing each other.'

'Only as friends. It's nothing more than that.'

'If you say so, dear.' Evelyn straightened her Sunday hat, frowning as she peered into the mirror propped up against the dresser. 'I really do need a new hat. I think this one has seen better days.'

'I see Simon from time to time only because I have to keep on good terms with everyone in the village. It's a teacher's duty. You know that, Mum.'

Evelyn turned and smiled at her daughter.

'I do, but you have to admit that you have some influence. He did take down that gate when you asked him, didn't he?'

Rowan was beginning to wonder about that. From her mother's window she could see the length of Front Street all the way to the harbour. She could also see the gap where the gate had been.

She remembered the look on Clett Drummond's face as his old Jeep shot past her yesterday on the road to Balcreggan House. Had Simon relented because of pressure from his tenant farmer?

'Mum, did you happen to see Simon's men take the gate away yesterday?'

Evelyn swung round.

'Come to think of it, I didn't. But it was down by early evening, because Dolly rang to tell me.'

Rowan froze. So all the time she had been with Simon and his mother, persuading him (as she had thought) to remove the gate, he had already done so! Why hadn't he said so? Why allow her to go babbling on, when all the while he must have been laughing at her?

A stab of anger swelled inside her as she and Evelyn walked to church. By the time they reached the little village church anger had grown into rage. Simon and his mother had made a fool of her.

She spotted the pair of them as soon as she walked into the church. Simon, his head down, seemed to be flicking though the pages of the hymn sheet. Beside him, the erect figure of his mother was dressed in a dark-green woollen coat with a hat of exactly the same shade of green. What a smug pair they made, Rowan thought unkindly.

There was no sign of Clett Drummond, but then she had hardly expected to see him in church. He hadn't struck her as a religious man. Annie Moncrief was there, and beside her sat two little girls whom Rowan took to be Clett's daughters, Charlotte and Poppy.

She could only see them from the back, so could only register that one had long, straight, fair hair, the same colour as her father's, and the other, smaller girl's short hair was a tangle of chestnut.

Looking around Rowan realised that the church seemed fuller than usual. She wondered why. As a result, it took longer to file out of the church after the service, as the Rev. Douglas Ritchie's usual practice was to shake hands and share a few words with each of his flock.

St Stephen's was in the heart of the village, set back from road that ran along the waterfront. People were gathering outside as usual, chatting in groups before dispersing to their various hones to enjoy the Sunday roast dinner ritual. She knew that, at that moment, there was also a joint of meat in her mother's oven, slowly cooking for their lunch.

'Ah, Rowan — and Mrs Fairlie.' Simon Fraser was striding towards them, arm outstretched in greeting. 'You look as elegant as ever, Mrs Fairlie.'

Rowan was dismayed to see her mother was actually blushing at Simon's attentions.

'I see you took the gate down after all, Simon.'

Just for a second Rowan thought she saw a glint of anger there, but the next second they were sparkling as he smiled back.

'You're very persuasive, Rowan.' He beamed at both of them, pausing to look back at Geraldine, who was hovering in the background, clearly impatient to be gone.

'We hope you can join us for lunch back at the house.'

Rowan could see Evelyn was itching to accept, but Rowan could think of nothing worse than an afternoon of polite small talk with Simon, when all she really wanted to do was to scream at him for the way he had treated her.

Evelyn's eyes slid to her daughter as she registered the almost imperceptible shake of Rowan's head.

'We would have loved to accept your kind invitation, but we already have a meal waiting for us at home.' She checked her watch. 'Which will be ruined if we don't hurry along!'

As they said their goodbyes and Simon turned away, Rowan caught the fury in his eyes. There it was again. Simon Fraser didn't like being refused.

They had turned down to the waterside and were heading along in the direction of the cottage when there was a call from behind them.

'Evelyn, I thought I'd missed you after church!'

Annie Moncrief hurried towards them, her two young charges following.

Rowan's gaze fell on the girls, who returned her smile with blank stares.

'Come along, you two.' Annie waved a hand at them. 'May I introduce Miss Charlotte and Miss Poppy Drummond?'

Rowan marked the formal introduction with amusement. Clearly she had worked too long in the Big House!

The girls stepped forward reluctantly. Rowan shook hands with them.

'It's nice to meet you both. Your father tells me that you're coming to our school.'

They scowled but said nothing.

Annie gave them a little push of encouragement.

'Oh, come on, you two. You know you'll love it once you're there. Think of all those new friends you will make here in Balcreggan.' She looked up at

Rowan. 'Isn't that right, Miss Fairlie?'

Rowan gave an encouraging nod.

'The reason I stopped you was to invite you to join us for Sunday lunch up at Ballinbrae. That is, Mr Drummond has asked me to invite you both.' She smiled. 'Please say you'll come, because if you don't, I don't know what I'll do with all that food.' She glanced fondly at the girls, who actually giggled. 'There are only so many roast beef sandwiches a girl can eat in a week!'

Two invitations to lunch, in as many minutes! But this one sounded decidedly more appealing.

'The very man!' Annie nodded along the front to where a familiar dusty Jeep was heading their way. 'Here's Mr Drummond now.'

The two little girls' faces became animated and they waved excitedly as their father approached. Clett parked across the road and jumped out. Rowan felt an inexplicable flurry of excitement as the tall figure came towards them.

He held out his arms and the girls ran to him, laughing.

'I was just telling Evelyn and Rowan here that they're invited up to the farm for lunch.' Annie smiled.

Clett switched his attention from his daughters to the two women and gave a funny little bow.

'We would be honoured if you would join us.'

Rowan knew her mother was ready to take her cue from her daughter. They had already refused Simon's invitation.

Clett looked at Rowan.

'I thought it would give Charlotte and Poppy a chance to get acquainted with their teacher in more familiar surroundings.'

She hesitated, but only for a split second.

'We'd love to accept.' She turned to Evelyn. 'Wouldn't we, Mum?'

Evelyn looked unsure but nodded.

'Would half an hour from now suit you?' he asked.

'That would be just fine.'

'That was interesting,' Evelyn said, as they set off for the cottage.

'Yes, two invitations in the same day.'

'Actually, I meant how you accepted so readily, when you'd refused Simon.'

Rowan could feel her face growing hot.

'You heard what Mr Drummond said, Mum. He wants his daughters to get to know me before they come to school in the morning.' She was aware that her mother was still looking at her in a doubtful way. 'It makes good sense. You said yourself that the family had been through a bad time. Anything that makes things a bit easier for those two children is fine by me.'

She left her mother at the cottage and headed up the hill to the school to collect her car. Strolling across the fields to Ballinbrae would be nothing to her, but she couldn't expect her mother to undertake the same trek.

Later, as Rowan pulled up alongside

61

Clett's Jeep at Ballinbrae, Evelyn stared around her.

'I haven't been here for . . . ' Evelyn's brow creased as she counted back the years 'Not since before your dad died.' Her gaze was fixed on the far field. 'We used to have fireworks parties up here on Guy Fawkes Night. The whole village came.' Evelyn's eyes were shining. 'And bonfires! Do you remember the bonfires, Rowan?'

Rowan nodded.

'Dad used to let me go with him to collect branches from the woods to help build the bonfire.'

A tear glistened in her mother's eyes.

'Those were good days.'

The farmhouse door opened and Clett came out. He'd changed from the crumpled checked shirt and mud-stained jeans he'd been wearing earlier. The chunky, cream fisherman's sweater suited him.

'We're all in the sitting-room. Just come through.'

Evelyn gave a little gasp of pleasure

as she looked round.

'You haven't changed it. It's just as I remember!'

That wasn't true. The room had changed. The walls were a new pale grey, and there were paintings of Highland scenes that looked expensive. But Evelyn was right about one thing. The basic ambience of the room was exactly the same — more comfortable than trendy.

She approved.

Charlotte and Poppy were stretched out in front of the fire, each reading a book. They barely glanced up to acknowledge the new arrivals.

'Enid Blyton?' Rowan crouched down beside them. 'She was one of my favourite authors when I was little. Which do you have?'

Charlotte held up a Famous Five adventure.

Poppy scrambled to her feet, her copper curls bobbing.

'I've got 'The Mystery Of The Hidden House' and I've almost finished it!'

'Great!' Rowan accepted the book and flicked through the pages. 'I remember this one.'

For a moment Poppy looked impressed by this new young teacher who didn't look like a teacher at all. But as she sat with the others at the big table at the far end of the room, Mrs Moncrief's roast beef dinner in front of her, she merely toyed with her food. She glanced across at her sister, who was also staring gloomily at her plate, jabbing at her roast potatoes with little enthusiasm.

'This is just about the best roast beef I've ever tasted, Annie,' Evelyn said. 'You must let me have the recipe.'

Rowan knew there was no finer cook in the whole village than her own mother, but the comment had the desired effect. Annie, whose worried face had been watching the girls, now beamed at the visitors from across the table.

'You're very lucky to have Annie,' Evelyn told Clett, who had also been watching his two sullen daughters.

But he merely nodded.

Rowan's heart went out to the little family. She wondered why he had decided to uproot them all from their familiar surroundings in Glasgow. A Highland village was a very different place from a busy city, and on top of all that the girls had to endure the trauma of starting a new school.

Children were resilient, she reminded herself. Their father was a different matter. He looked no happier than his daughters. And now there was this issue with Simon. Clett Drummond had made an enemy, when what he probably needed most was a friend.

He caught her looking at him.

'I'm sorry. We invite you both here for lunch and then ignore you. We're not very good hosts, are we, girls?'

'There's apple pie and custard if anyone wants it.' Annie jumped to her feet in an effort to lighten the awkward atmosphere. She smiled fondly at the two little girls. 'I'm sure you two could manage a bit of that.'

Poppy actually grinned and nodded to Annie. Charlotte raised her eyes and her mouth pursed into an acceptance.

Rowan moved to help clear the table but her mother waved her back.

'I'll help Annie to do this. And you girls can come through to help me find some plates.'

They left the room. Now was as good a time as any to ask what had been on Rowan's mind all morning.

'I see you managed to persuade Simon Fraser to remove his gate.'

She tried to study Clett's eyes as closely as she had Simon's, but their intensity was distracting, and she looked away. But not before she saw triumph in them.

'He saw reason.' Clett reached across the table for the bottle of red wine and topped up Rowan's glass. The subject was apparently closed.

'You'll find my girls hard work, I'm afraid.' He sighed. 'I wanted you to see what you are up against.'

Rowan sipped her wine.

'It's likely Charlotte and Poppy are still missing their mum, and very natural. These things take time.'

'And now I've uprooted them from everything they've ever known.' He shook his head. 'I thought a completely new start would be good for all of us — help us to forget.'

'The girls may not want to forget. It's still early days, remember.' She strove to inject a positive tone into her voice. 'But it will get better . . . I promise you.'

He looked away, and the sadness she saw in his eyes melted her heart. Clett Drummond had obviously adored his dead wife.

New Beginnings

Rowan checked her diary. She had suggested to Clett Drummond that nine-thirty would be a good time to bring his daughters to school. By then she would be free to show all three of them around. She felt a tiny stab of pleasure. It was good to have more children coming to the school. These days, young people, who couldn't find work in the area usually left to seek employment further afield. Some, like her, came back to Balcreggan, but were in the minority. A quiet life in a peaceful Highland village didn't suit everybody, no matter how beautiful.

The morning register check satisfactorily completed, Rowan nodded to Helen to look after her class and made her way to her office.

The expensive fountain pen Simon had bought her for Christmas lay on the desk. She picked it up thoughtfully. She wished she'd handled things differently when he'd invited her to accompany him to the Highland Ball.

In one way, her mother was right — Simon Fraser was a very eligible man, both handsome and rich. But people were wary of him. Talk flew when locals gathered in the pub. Where had the man come from? What did a businessman — a property developer at that — know about running an estate like Balcreggan?

Rowan was aware of the mistrust and it annoyed her. Simon Fraser at least deserved a chance. She remembered that he'd said he had booked two rooms at the Inverlochy Hotel. Had she been misjudging him?

The sound of Clett Drummond's farm Jeep drawing up in the school's small car park made her look up. She watched him help his daughters jump down.

The girls were dressed immaculately in pristine grey pleated skirts, white polo shirts, red cardigans, grey tights and shiny black shoes.

She saw the disgruntled frowns as they both looked over the school building.

She came out to greet them and led the way into the school and along the short corridor into her office. The girls took up their places on either side of their father, watching her with large apprehensive eyes. They obviously didn't want to be here.

Rowan tried to put herself in their place. She remembered her own sadness when her father died. She'd been inconsolable. Surely losing a mother when you were still so little was even more traumatic. It had been just over a year since Mrs Drummond's accident. And now they had been brought here, to this new place where they knew no-one.

Small wonder they were apprehensive!

Clett gave their details and information, looking as apprehensive as the girls. Rowan made a note of everything. Then she laid down her pen and smiled at them. They stared glumly back. Charlotte, she noted, had her father's blonde hair, and there was no doubting where Poppy's beautiful green eyes had come from. But Charlotte's deep blue eyes and her sister's mop of bouncy copper curls must have come from their mother. Rowan realised that Rachel Drummond must have been a very beautiful woman — and for some reason that knowledge unsettled her.

'Right, Charlotte and Poppy,' she started brightly. 'You know my name, and you can come to me if anything is worrying you. Is there anything you want to ask?'

'Our last school had a swimming pool,' Charlotte asked. 'Have you got a swimming pool?'

'I'm afraid we don't. But the beach isn't very far away, and lots of people go swimming there in the summer.'

Charlotte stared at her, obviously not impressed.

Rowan gave an encouraging smile.

'You're going to make lots of new friends here. And in no time at all I'm sure you'll get to like us.'

Clett looked up and spoke.

'Miss Fairlie's right, girls. You really will like it here.'

Poppy took her father's hand, her beautiful green eyes brimming with tears. Charlotte fixed Rowan with a defiant stare.

'We don't want to come to this school. Poppy and I want to go home.'

Clett gathered both girls in his arms.

'I'm sure you won't be saying that when I come to collect you later.' He kissed each of them in turn before releasing them and standing up. But before he turned away Rowan caught such an expression of such sadness and loss on his face that it took her breath away. Swallowing a lump in her throat she stood up.

'I expect you would like to see round your new school.' She went to the door and held it open.

In the school hall, which also doubled as the canteen and gym, she pointed to the climbing equipment stored at the far end.

'Your landlord, Mr Fraser, bought those for the school,' she told Clett.

His brows came down and he surveyed the equipment with a hostile glare.

The rest of the short tour ended at the classroom door and twenty-four pairs of eyes looked up as Poppy and Charlotte made their reluctant entrance. Helen Gemmel came forward, smiling.

'Hello, you two! We've saved a couple of desks for you right here in the front row.'

Rowan saw the girls cast wary glances over the rest of the class before sliding reluctantly into their places. She turned to Clett.

'They'll be fine now. Just leave them with us.'

She followed him to the door, taking one final glance back at two solemn, pale, little faces in the sea of cheery, rosy-cheeked Highland ones.

They returned to the office for Clett to complete the final remaining registration form. A lock of bright hair fell over his forehead as he bent to write his signature. When he looked up his eyes were serious.

'What interest does Simon Fraser have in this school?'

The question took her by surprise.

'He doesn't — not officially. I mean, he's not on the board of governors, or anything like that. He's just a very generous man.' She looked up and met his gaze. 'Why do you ask?'

He shrugged.

'I saw you two talking down by the harbour that day.'

'That conversation was personal,' she said, more sharply than she had intended. 'Mr Fraser and I are friends.'

He nodded.

'Sorry. I didn't mean to pry.'

Outside in the corridor she touched Clett's arm.

'All children are apprehensive when they start a new school.'

He was looking about as crestfallen as his daughters, and she had an urge to put her arms around him. The feeling shocked her and she took an involuntary step back.

Clett noticed it and took it as a sign of dismissal.

'I'll leave my daughters in your capable hands, then.'

Rowan smiled up into his worried green eyes.

'They'll be fine. Don't fret about them.'

She waited until he was out of the door then went back to her office and watched from the window until she saw the farm Jeep drive out of the school gates. This day felt like a new beginning for more than just the Drummond family.

But why had the mere mention of Simon's name upset Clett Drummond? She didn't know, but she would be interested in finding out.

*　*　*

Charlotte didn't settle into Balcreggan Primary as well as Rowan had predicted. In fact, she didn't settle at all. Poppy, on the other hand, was more outgoing and made friends more easily. The same could not be said for Charlotte who appeared determined to remain aloof from everything. She ignored any friendly approaches from the other children in her class, and they eventually stopped bothering to speak to her.

A Chance Meeting

On the day of the Highland Ball, Rowan was on her way to Inverness. She hadn't been on a decent shopping trip in ages. As she drove across the Kessock Bridge she tried to think back on how long it had been, and was shocked to realise it was more than three months ago, when she had gone for Christmas presents.

This was to be another gift-buying excursion, for a birthday present for her niece, Hannah. She had hoped her mother might join her today, but Evelyn had called off at the last minute, explaining today it was her turn for the Meals On Wheels run.

She parked in the multi storey car park she always used when she came to the city. It linked up with a new shopping mall, which she walked through on her way out to the main street. The last time she was here the shops had been festooned in tinsel.

She found a café opposite the castle and sat sipping a latté while she planned her day. She knew exactly which gift she was planning to buy for Hannah, and decided to do that first. With the package safely tucked away in her bag, she set off exploring.

Walking by the river she noticed a new bistro. The windows in the upstairs restaurant were wide and looked directly onto the footbridge across the river. It would be a lovely spot for her to have lunch later.

At the far end of the road she turned right, heading for an old church she knew had been turned into a second-hand bookshop. Rowan had found the place by accident a year earlier, and loved its eclectic mix of old and new. Amongst its rows of shelves the persistent browser could find original copies of tomes that covered every stage of Scotland's history and culture. This section was her particular favourite. She was fascinated to read about how people lived in the 18th and 19th centuries, how they dressed, what they ate and what kind of dwellings they lived in. She'd already used information gleaned from books she'd bought here as the basis of some school projects.

Trailing a finger along the rows of volumes as she browsed the shelves Rowan was startled by a voice speaking her name. She spun round and found herself looking into a pair of familiar green eyes.

'Mr Drummond!'

'I'm sorry. I didn't mean to startle you.' He waved an arm around indicating the rows of dusty books. 'I see we have an interest in common, Miss Fairlie.'

Rowan smiled back at the wide green eyes. Was he teasing her?

'Have you found anything interesting?'

'No, but then I'm really not searching for anything in particular. I just like to browse around old places.'

'Did you find this place by accident, too?' She was struggling to keep up this conversation. But Clett Drummond really was the last person she would have expected to encounter in this old bookstore.

He looked at his watch.

'I was thinking of finding somewhere to have a drink. Can I persuade you to join me?'

She could have told him she'd already had a coffee, but if she did that he would walk away and it suddenly became important that he shouldn't do that.

'That would be very welcome.'

They left together and began walking back into the town centre. She had to quicken her step to keep up with him, and she realised that he knew exactly where he was going. Clett Drummond was clearly no stranger to Inverness.

She slid him a glance.

'You seem to know the city quite well.'

'What makes you think that?'

She shrugged.

'You know where you're going.'

'I have business interests here.' He made no attempt to elaborate on his statement.

Suddenly, and without warning, he stopped.

'Where are my manners? I haven't even asked if you have a preference about where we should go.'

'That depends on whether you want an alcoholic drink or not.' She studied him for a second. 'You look like a man who wants a pint.'

Suddenly he was smiling back at her, a proper smile that crinkled the corners of his mouth and made his eyes twinkle. All at once the world seemed a nicer place.

'What a very perceptive young woman you are.' There was more than a hint of mischief in the pale eyes. 'As it happens, I know just the place.'

A few minutes later they came to a stop outside what Rowan had thought was a shop. Through the window she could see a mix of wooden tables and assorted chairs and benches. Inside, Clett pointed towards an alcove where a couple of battered-looking red leather armchairs flanked a low scrubbed wooden table.

'There?'

Rowan nodded and made for the alcove as Clett headed to the bar to order their drinks. She watched him as he waited his turn. There was no sign today of the well-worn brown leather jacket he always wore in Balcreggan. It had been replaced with a green tweed jacket and beige slacks. His shoes, too, looked expensive. Clett Drummond would be hard pushed to be taken for a farmer today.

Rowan glanced down at her own clothes. She'd swapped her skirts and smart suits for a white T-shirt, denim jacket and stretch jeans tucked into high brown leather boots. They had almost reversed identities!

'How on earth did you find this place?' she asked when he returned with their drinks.

'Live music.' He nodded to posters advertising performances by the cream of Inverness's musical talent. 'I'm a fan. Admittedly the place is a bit quirky, but I like that.'

Rowan glanced around the dimly lit room, taking in the candles on the tables, a couple of extraordinary chandeliers and an enormous scarred oaken door propped up against a wall. The thing looked so ancient it could have come from some mediaeval castle.

'It's not short on character, I'll grant you that!'

She wondered if this was the right time to ask how he came to know Inverness so well. It was none of her business, of course, but she was curious.

'I thought you were brand new to the Highlands, but that's not true, is it?' she ventured.

He sat back, in no hurry to reply.

'I have an accountant here, and I had business with him today.'

An accountant. She wasn't expecting that. But, then, why wouldn't a farmer have an accountant? He saw the brief question in her eye.

'I was based in Glasgow before coming north, but I've had business interests here for some time now. Still do.'

Rowan glanced at the long smooth fingers that showed no evidence of calluses. These were not the work-worn hands of a man who made his living from the land. Her eyes flew open.

'You're not really a farmer at all, are you?'

She remembered what he'd said the day she had gone to find him at Ballinbrae, to try to dissuade him from rushing down to the harbour and pulling down Simon Fraser's gate. At the time, the words would have gone over her head. Her only concern was to stop Clett and the village men getting themselves into any trouble.

He'd said he wanted to buy the farm. Buy it, not lease it.

'You're right. I'm not a farmer, not in the way you mean. But I want to be.'

He went on to describe his early upbringing on the Drummond family farm in Ayrshire.

'I loved working on the land, and would have been more than happy to have gone on doing that. But when my father died the tenancy of the farm went to my older brother, Stephen . . . as it should. I'd always known that would happen, but when it actually did it gave me a jolt. I took myself off to Glasgow and got a place at a technical college, and learned how to build things.'

He swilled the dregs of his drink around the bottom of his glass and glanced back towards the bar.

'Are you hungry? They do great stovies here!'

Rowan would have preferred to hear the rest of the story, but she suspected he had interrupted himself on purpose. She nodded.

'Stovies sound great, but it's my

treat.' She reached for her bag, making to stand up but he waved her down.

'I wouldn't hear of it,' he said, and the smile went all the way to his wonderful eyes, making them shine. She wished he would do that more often.

'That's very kind of you, Mr Drummond, but I can buy my own lunch, you know.'

'Call it thanks for listening to my ramblings.'

As they waited for their food to arrive Rowan hoped he would return to his story, but he didn't. He surprised her instead by asking about his daughters.

It brought her back to earth with a jolt. She was forgetting she was a teacher, and that the man opposite — no matter how attractive he might be — was the father of two of her pupils. She straightened.

'The girls are settling in fine.'

But was that true? She certainly had no worries about Poppy, the extrovert sister who seemed to have no trouble making new friends.

Charlotte was another story. Rowan was beginning to feel a little worried about the girl. She showed little interest in her lessons and went out of her way to reject any friendly gestures from the other children.

'Actually, that's not right. To be more precise, Poppy is settling well, but Charlotte is still reserved.'

He nodded.

'Charlotte is a loner. I'm afraid she takes after me.' He looked up and forced a grin. 'She doesn't trust anybody. Even in Glasgow she didn't have as many friends as Poppy. I did think this move would have been good for her, but now I'm not so sure. They had a good life in Glasgow — too good, some might say.'

Rowan raised a questioning eyebrow.

'My daughters were spoiled. Clothes, treats, toys . . . they got everything they wanted.'

Was he talking about his late wife?

'That's no crime, Clett. Little ones deserve to be spoiled, sometimes.'

If he noticed she'd used his first name he didn't react to it. But then he looked up and their eyes locked.

Rowan felt a connection so strong that she almost gripped the sides of her chair to steady herself. For a few seconds neither of them spoke.

'You think I'm being too hard on my daughters?'

She leaned towards him.

'Of course I don't think that. It's obvious how much you adore Charlotte and Poppy.' She gave him a hesitant smile. 'And equally obvious how much they love you.'

His shoulders rose in a shrug.

'I had this notion of sharing some of my own childhood values with them — the land, the animals. It hasn't worked out that way.'

Rowan laughed, shaking her head.

'Don't underestimate your daughters. Children have a habit of surprising you when you least expect it. And Balcreggan is a wonderful place to grow up in.' She put up her hands to indicate herself. 'It never did me any harm!'

Clett was looking at her in a searching way.

'I can see that.'

Their food arrived and they ate in silence. Rowan had learned more about him in the last hour than she had in the previous two weeks. Maybe what he'd told her would help her to better understand his two daughters, especially Charlotte. She wasn't really worried about Poppy. After an initial wary start the little girl seemed to be settling happily into her new school. Her sunny nature had already won her friends and Rowan noticed that she was often at the centre of any group activity in the playground.

The older girl was different, much more reserved than her sister, a loner who seemed to shun the attempts of other children to befriend her. Eventually they would stop trying.

But if Clett was right and Charlotte's attitude to the others was born out of her wish to move back to Glasgow then it might explain why she made no effort to make friends.

She'd been so deep in her own thoughts that she hadn't realised Clett had been talking to her. He gave her a quizzical look.

'Am I boring you?'

Rowan shook her head, embarrassed. She glanced at her watch and began to collect her things.

'As pleasant as this has been, I really must get back.'

Clett stood up with a look of disappointment in his eyes.

'Do you really have to go? It's still early, and my daughters are not the only ones who need a friend.'

Once again Rowan had to remind herself that this man was the father of two of her pupils. Yet his reluctance to let her go suggested he wanted to put the relationship on a more personal footing. Or was she imagining that?

She gave him her brightest smile, patting her stomach.

'I suppose it would be a good idea to

walk off some of that food.'

They left the pub and began to stroll through the Inverness streets, unaware that eyes followed them — eyes which were steely grey and narrowed in anger. Simon Fraser was standing at the first-floor window of the Inverness office of his company, Highland Properties . . .

*　*　*

Unaware they were being watched, Clett and Rowan strolled together through the town centre, past the tartan shops, the pubs and cafés, eventually reaching the castle.

They turned down by the river and wandered along the banks until they reached an area of woodland paths and footbridges known to the locals as The Islands. They passed a group of men in dark suits, crisp shirts and ties — delegates from some business conference at the nearby Eden Court Theatre complex.

'You mentioned business interests in Inverness.' She glanced up at him but his face gave away nothing. 'Is that all in the past as well?'

'I run an engineering company in Glasgow. Used to run,' he corrected himself. 'I sold up before we moved up here.'

'You gave up an engineering company to become a tenant farmer in Balcreggan?' Her voice was incredulous.

He laughed.

'Not a great business move, eh? But it wasn't quite as drastic as that. I had already established a satellite division here in Inverness.' He nodded across the city. 'It's out on the industrial estate and is being run efficiently by Gary Ballantyne, my manager.'

'What does this business of yours make?'

'The same as we did in Glasgow. We provide custom-built steel structures, but in the city we were involved in the construction of school buildings, shopping malls and other public buildings.

In this area it's more likely to be farm buildings.'

'You built shopping malls?'

'Very small ones. But we were doing all right. I sold the business as a going concern to move up here.'

Rowan put her hands to her head.

'I don't understand. If you already have a thriving business in Inverness, why haven't you bought a big house here and stayed here to run your business. What on earth are you doing in Balcreggan?'

Had she overstepped the mark? It was none of her business where he wanted to live.

'It was Balcreggan that started the whole thing off. One of our competitors in Glasgow had been at me for some time to sell up to him. I saw the advert in a newspaper for a tenant farmer at Ballinbrae, and applied, thinking I might be able to buy the farm. As I suspect you already know, Simon Fraser refused to sell. But I'm still working on that.'

Rowan shook her head.

'You're a man of many surprises, Mr Drummond.'

He smiled at her.

'My name's Clett.'

A Thief

At the end of the little stretch of garden that was allotted to the schoolhouse Rowan could see the first splurge of yellow. She had been looking forward to the appearance of the first crocuses. She usually felt a little surge of pleasure when Mondays came around, having mapped out a schedule of projects for the coming week. But that hadn't happened this weekend and she fought back a guilty feeling that she was somehow neglecting her young charges.

It was Clett Drummond's fault. Her mind had been a maelstrom of questions since Inverness. He'd told her so much about his past, and at the same time nothing at all about the important things. He had never once talked about his late wife, Rachel. Maybe even the mention of his lost love was too much for him. For some unaccountable reason that had brought a black cloud down on Rowan's day.

She stared glumly at her reflection in the mirror as she slicked on a touch of lipstick. Outside she could hear the first of the children arriving in the playground, and when she glanced out she saw that Charlotte and Poppy were amongst the early arrivals. Hannah and Josh were also there.

Poppy, in her padded pink coat, was skipping in their direction. Charlotte hung back, reluctant to follow her sister. Her head was down and she was stubbing the toe of her red shoe against the playground tarmac. Her body language said everything. Charlotte did not want to be here.

Rowan's heart went out to her. She'd been keeping a special eye on the little girl. Until now Rowan had kept her distance, but perhaps it was time for some one-to-one attention with young Charlotte. There had to be something more going on here.

The memory of Inverness was still

ringing in her head, but she would think about that later. For now she had to concentrate on Clett's daughter, to find a way of helping her to make friends and settle into the school.

She ran over what he'd told her. She knew about the engineering firm he had sold in the hopes of buying Ballinbrae Farm. She had no idea how prosperous his business had been, but she imagined that he and his family had lived in some style in Glasgow. She was picturing a big house in one of the city's sought-after suburbs. The image she conjured up of Rachel was of a stylishly beautiful woman with perfectly manicured nails and immaculate designer clothes.

She gave herself a shake. Was she jealous of this man's poor, dead wife? How horrible. She forced her mind back to Charlotte. If that was the kind of lifestyle the family had had in Glasgow, then no wonder she were finding it hard to settle in here. Poppy, more gregarious, was making the best of an unwanted situation. Charlotte was more complex. Rowan bit her lip as she watched the playground slowly fill with children. She would have to find a way to help this child.

It was going-home time before she came up with the idea. Her sister, Shona, had roped her into baking for Hannah's eighth-birthday tea on Wednesday. She popped down that evening to discuss the plans, and casually asked whom her niece had invited to her party.

There would be ten little guests in all, she learned. Hannah's eyes lit up as she reeled off all the names of her friends.

'And Poppy,' she finished breathlessly. Rowan smiled.

'What about Charlotte? Is she not your friend, too?'

Hannah's little face took on an expression of horror.

'I don't want her. She tells lies!'

'That's not a nice thing to say, Hannah.'

'Fibs, then. Charlotte tells fibs.'

Rowan looked away, hiding her frown. She wasn't about to encourage her niece to tell tales on a fellow classmate. But if Charlotte had a reputation of being dishonest, making new friends at school could be harder work than Rowan had thought.

Later, when Hannah and Josh had gone to bed, Rowan and Shona were discussing the birthday party.

'I heard you talking about the Drummond girls. The little one, Poppy, is an angel. All the kids love her. But the other one . . . she's a sad little thing, isn't she?'

'I'm worried about her, Shona. I know I shouldn't discuss any of the children out of school, but this little girl concerns me. She seems to be doing all she can to alienate everyone.'

Shona sighed.

'I feel bad about Hannah inviting Poppy and not Charlotte.'

'Yes. Just imagine how hurt Charlotte must be feeling. I don't suppose you can find a way to persuade Hannah to include her?'

Shona shook her head.

'I suggested it . . . ' She bit her lip. 'Look, Rowan, I don't know if I should say anything about this. It's only children talking, but . . . '

'Tell me, Shona. Whatever it is, I can't help if I don't know!'

'You heard Hannah talking about Charlotte telling lies?'

Rowan nodded.

'Well, according to them — Hannah and her friends, I mean — Charlotte has been stealing.'

Rowan froze.

'Surely not! Have they said why they believe this?' True or not, this was a potentially explosive situation. And if it was true, then it was indeed serious. Rowan knew she would have to investigate it. Stealing could often be a child's cry for help, and Charlotte certainly did need help.

She looked at her sister.

'I don't have to tell you to keep this

to yourself, Shona.'

Shona stared back, annoyed.

'Of course! I've no intention of repeating it, but children do talk to their parents . . . '

Rowan's thoughts were in a whirl as she climbed the hill back up to the schoolhouse. She'd have a word with Helen in the morning. And Clett, what could she say to him? But she was getting ahead of herself. She would see what Helen had to say before she took any action.

⋆ ⋆ ⋆

'Actually, I was going to mention it. I did catch a snatch of something in the playground last week,' Helen admitted when tackled.

'Why on earth didn't you tell me, Helen?'

'I'm sorry, Rowan. I wasn't sure what to do. I didn't want to get the child into trouble until I knew more. It could have been just a grudge one of the children

101

was harbouring against Charlotte. She isn't exactly friendly towards any of them.'

Rowan let out a long, heartfelt sigh.

'Tell me what exactly you have heard.'

'Little things have been going missing. Someone's favourite pencil, a rubber, gloves, a scarf and even a lunchbox.'

Rowan stared at her, mouth open.

'I can't believe you didn't tell me about this!'

Helen hung her head.

'I'm so sorry.'

'Go and fetch the key to Charlotte's locker. I want this settled right now!'

Rowan's hand shook as she turned the little key in the lock. The metal door swung back to reveal a stack of goods. Everything Helen had mentioned was here, as well as other things. There was a tiny silver bracelet very similar to one Rowan had seen little Emily Mitchell wearing. Charlotte must have been busy for days to have accumulated a haul like this.

She closed the door and relocked it, tucking the key into her pocket, then walked slowly back to her office to consider her next move.

Clett would have to be told what his daughter had been up to, but right now it was her responsibility. She would have to handle the situation carefully. She didn't believe for a minute that Charlotte was a committed thief. Surely this was a cry for help?

A sudden wail from outside her office window sent Rowan hurrying to the playground. Emily Mitchell, with her distinctive cloud of copper coloured hair and freckled face wasn't hard to spot.

She sat whimpering in the middle of the playground, hugging a grazed knee as the other children crowded round.

Charlotte, too, had witnessed Emily's fall but she held back, watching the little drama from the sidelines. On an impulse Rowan waved her forward.

'Come and help me, Charlotte,' she called. 'Help me take Emily back to the office. We have to get this poor knee cleaned up.'

Charlotte's shocked stare went from one to the other and she drew back.

Emily looked up, the huge tears glistening in her blue eyes suddenly brimming over.

'Want Poppy to help me.'

But Rowan was firm, nodding to Charlotte to take Emily's arm and help her classmate to hobble back into the school building.

Inside the office Charlotte watched with wary eyes as Rowan gently bathed Emily's wound.

'Can you fetch the First Aid box?' She nodded towards the cupboard where it was kept.

Charlotte collected the box and handed it to Rowan, who selected a plaster which she then offered to Charlotte.

'Can you put this on Emily's knee while I wash my hands, please?' She tried to sound as matter of fact as she could.

'But I might do it wrong!' Now it was

Charlotte who wailed in alarm.

'I'll show you. We can do it together, if that's all right with Emily?'

Emily gave a reluctant shrug.

As Rowan helped Charlotte to apply the plaster she spoke casually.

'It's not been your week, has it, Emily? Miss Gemmel told me about your bracelet.'

Charlotte's head shot up and her face turned puce as Emily's tears began to flow again.

'It was a present from my nan,' she whimpered. 'I was going to keep it for ever and now I've lost it!'

Charlotte was now looking decidedly wretched.

Rowan forced a hopeful note into her voice.

'Don't worry, Emily. Maybe we'll still find it. Lost things do sometimes turn up, you know.'

Emily dabbed at her eyes with the tissue Rowan offered and gave a weak, tremulous smile that this time included Charlotte.

'I think I hear Miss Gemmel ringing the bell for end of break. Will you take Emily back to the classroom, please, Charlotte? I'll be through in a minute.'

Charlotte's eyes remained cast to the floor as the pair of them left the room.

Rowan felt guilty that her mention of the missing bracelet had upset the child, but she crossed her fingers, hoping for the best.

And over the next few days every one of the missing items mysteriously turned up in the desks of their owners, causing much excitement.

Rowan kept a close eye on Charlotte. One thing was certain. Returning the property had not seemed to make the little girl any happier . . .

* * *

There was surprise in Clett Drummond's voice when he answered Rowan's call. But he had to be told what Charlotte had done, even if she had since returned the property. The

106

situation was a delicate one. Rowan could hear the raucous cries of seagulls down the phone and realised he must be out in the fields. At this time of year he would be preparing the land for seeding.

'I wonder if we could have a chat sometime today?'

'Is it the girls? Has something happened?' The alarm in his voice startled her.

She kept her tone casual.

'Well, actually, there is something that's been worrying me. It concerns Charlotte, but I don't think we should discuss it on the phone. Can you come here later?'

They needed to talk.

It was dark when Clett's Jeep pulled into the school's small parking area. By the time he had switched off the engine and got out Rowan had opened the door, and light was flooding out on to the path.

'This all sounds very mysterious. Should I be worried?' His face showed that he clearly already was.

She indicated one of her comfortable armchairs and he sat down opposite, keeping his eyes on her face.

'It's a bit delicate,' she began.

Rowan watched Clett's eyes widen, first in confusion then in disbelief, as she recounted the details of his elder daughter's stealing spree.

'All the property has been returned,' she said, 'but we can't leave Charlotte with the idea that she can do things like this. We must at least talk to her about why she did it.' He was holding his head in his hands. Her heart went out to him. It wasn't fair. Families were supposed to be happy, but there was something at the heart of this one that seemed to be tearing them apart!

Rowan was not prepared for what happened next day. In the middle of a spelling lesson Charlotte's hand suddenly shot up. Assuming she wanted permission to leave the room, Rowan nodded to her. The girl stood up and marched to the front of the class.

'It was me,' she announced, her voice trembling. 'It was me that took the things. I didn't mean to, and I don't know why I did it.' She'd lost the battle to control her voice and it came out in a sob.

'I'm sorry!' she cried as she tore out of the room.

For a second nobody spoke. Poppy, in the middle of the front row was rubbing her eyes with her fists, tears coursing down her cheeks. Suddenly more children were crying in sympathy.

Once Rowan had managed to gain control of her class and comfort Poppy, she went to ask Helen to look after the class. She'd no idea where Charlotte had run off to, but she had to find her.

Charlotte's little red jacket was still on its peg, and Rowan's heart sank at the thought of the little girl wandering goodness knew where, outdoors, without a jacket on such a cold day.

Missing!

She definitely came into the play-ground, because I saw her. She may just have gone home, but I've got an uneasy feeling about this.' Helen's huge brown eyes were wide with alarm. 'Should we call the police?'

Rowan tried to control the torrent of thoughts that were rushing through her brain.

'Let's not panic just yet. But I will call the police if I don't find Charlotte within half an hour.' She was already heading for the door. 'I'll keep in touch and ring you the minute there's any news!'

She hurried out of the school playground, struggling into her jacket as she tore along the country road towards Ballinbrae Farm. She'd no idea if Charlotte would have come this way or not, but it seemed logical she wouldn't be brave enough to leave the village.

With its commanding position on the peninsula, Ballinbrae Farm was surrounded on three sides by water. The area was spectacularly beautiful, and in a few weeks it would be spring, when the hedgerows would be splurges of yellow broom. The musky scent always made Rowan feel nostalgic for her childhood.

She stopped suddenly, listening. Was that a muffled cry? The sound had come from the other side of the hedge. It could be an injured animal, or . . .

'Are you there, Charlotte? Is that you?'

'I'm through here.' The voice came through jerky sobs. 'Please help me. I can't get out!'

'I'm coming, Charlotte!' Rowan cried, frantically trying to find a gap in the dense hedge.

Then she saw one. It was tiny, but if she tried she could just about squeeze through.

Her hand flew to her mouth as she

saw the crumpled, bleeding form crouching in the ditch.

'Charlotte! Oh, Charlotte!'

The little girl drew back as Rowan approached.

'I'm not going back to school. You can't make me!'

Rowan's arms went round her. She could feel her frail body trembling with the sobs.

'You're safe now, Charlotte. I won't let anything happen to you, I promise.'

Charlotte looked up, her blue eyes still glistening with tears.

'I . . . I was going home,' she said, her words coming in gulps. 'Then I heard somebody coming, and squeezed through the hedge. It was prickly and it scratched my hands and face.' The tears were spilling over again. 'I didn't see the ditch, and I fell into it. I don't want to go back to school, Miss Fairlie. Please don't make me!'

Rowan hugged her close.

'Home is the only place you're going, young lady.'

'Not school?' Charlotte's great blue eyes were still brimming with tears.

Rowan shook her head and smiled.

'How does a glass of warm milk and a biscuit sound? I'm sure Mrs Moncrief will have some in your kitchen.'

'Can I have hot chocolate instead?' She slid Rowan a hopeful look. 'Poppy and I usually have that.'

'Hot chocolate it is, then.' She helped Charlotte struggle to her feet as she made a quick assessment of her injuries. She was scratched and bleeding and wet from the ditch, but thankfully everything seemed to be superficial.'

Charlotte allowed herself to be led along the edge of the field until they found a gate. Ballinbrae farm was less than a quarter of a mile along the quiet country road, but no vehicle passed as they made their slow progress.

Clett's housekeeper had seen their arrival from a window, and the door flew open as she rushed out to them.

'My heavens, the poor wee lassie.

Whatever's happened?' Annie Moncrief put an arm around Charlotte as she hurried them into the kitchen.

Annie scribbled Clett's mobile number on the back of a shopping list before marching Charlotte upstairs to change into warm, dry clothes and bathe her scratched face and hands. Rowan tapped in the number, but it took two attempts before Clett answered.

His voice was gruff. He obviously didn't appreciate being interrupted when he was out in the tractor.

She took a steadying breath before she spoke.

'Mr Drummond — Clett — it's Rowan Fairlie. There's nothing to worry about, but Charlotte has had a little . . . ' she struggled to find the least alarming word ' . . . adventure.'

'What adventure? Has Charlotte been hurt?'

Rowan could hear the alarm in his voice now and she was overcome by compassion for this man. He was struggling to bring up his two young daughters at a time when he must still be grieving for his wife.

'She's fine, really.' Rowan swallowed. 'There's too much to explain over the phone, but the main thing is she's safe.'

Clett wasn't convinced, and demanded to know what had happened to his daughter. Rowan kept the details to a minimum.

'When I realised she'd gone off I went to find her. She'd squeezed through a hedge and fallen into a rather boggy ditch, and was feeling more than a little sorry for herself when I found her.'

'Where is she now?'

'Here at Ballinbrae. Mrs Moncrief has taken her upstairs now to bathe her scratches and get her into some dry clothes . . . '

Clett didn't wait for her to finish the sentence.

'I'm on my way,' he said, and the phone went dead.

Five minutes later the kitchen door flew open and Clett burst in, bringing with him a blast of sharp sea air and the earthy smell the fields.

Rowan tried a reassuring smile.

'They're still upstairs, but I need to speak to you before Charlotte comes back.'

Over the next five minutes Rowan explained to Clett the events that had led up to his daughter taking flight. He looked away, his eyes glistening.

'This is all my fault,' he said, brokenly. 'I haven't been spending enough time with them.'

Rowan crossed the room to put a hand on his arm.

'You're wrong,' she said softly. 'Oh, I know the stealing was wrong, and so does Charlotte, now. But owning up to it in front of the whole class, as she did today was actually very brave.' She looked up and met his eyes. 'You should be proud of your little girl.'

They moved apart as they heard Annie and Charlotte coming back. Charlotte spoke in a wavering voice.

'I'm sorry, Dad. Am I in trouble?'

116

Clett opened his arms and his daughter rushed into them. He cradled her with such tenderness that Rowan had to swallow a lump in her throat. Over the child's head his eyes met hers.

'Thank you,' he mouthed.

Charlotte turned, eyes startled.

'I still don't have to go back to school with you, do I?'

The fear in her face melted Rowan's heart. She shook her head.

'That can wait till tomorrow. The important thing is that you know you did wrong, but you owned up to it and gave everybody their things back.' Charlotte nodded and Rowan could see her lip tremble.

Annie stepped in, beckoning Charlotte to follow her.

'Come away with me, lassie, and we'll see if those biscuits I've just baked will be cool enough to eat yet.'

Charlotte looked back and spoke in a barely audible voice.

'Thank you for finding me, Miss Fairlie.'

Clett's eyes were also on Rowan, and for an instant seemed to hold something more than gratitude.

'Just a minute, Rowan,' he said as she headed for the door. 'I'll give you a lift back to the school.' He waved away her protest. 'It's the least I can do.'

As they drove out of the yard Rowan faced him.

'How is Charlotte — in general, I mean? I'm worried that she doesn't seem to be settling in at school as well as Poppy. I don't think she is a very happy little girl.'

'She misses her mum,' he replied quietly, and there was so much sadness in his eyes that Rowan wished she hadn't brought up the subject.

'I'm sorry. I didn't mean to intrude. If there's anything I can do to help, anything at all, then just let me know.'

They'd reached the school's car park and she scrambled down from the Jeep before he could walk round to help her.

'I can't tell you now grateful I am.'

She felt herself colour at the compliment.

'I was just doing my job.'

'A bit more than that, I think. Anyway, I'm very grateful.'

Again Rowan felt that electric connection between them. She couldn't be imagining it!

★　★　★

Back at the classroom, Poppy was still looking upset when Rowan walked in. Rowan drew her aside.

'Charlotte's fine.' She smiled. 'I met her outside and took her home.'

That was enough detail for the time being.

When the class was assembled, Rowan told them how sorry Charlotte was about what she'd done.

Her class didn't appear entirely convinced.

'Charlotte doesn't like us.' It was Fiona Brown, an earnest little girl. 'She doesn't like any of us.'

Other young heads were nodding in agreement and Poppy was beginning to look tearful again.

'Of course Charlotte likes you! She likes all of you. But the thing is, she's shy.'

They still didn't look convinced.

'She stole our things.' Katie Crombie sniffed.

'She's so sorry about that.' Rowan frowned. 'It was like a kind of game to her. She didn't realise how upset it would make all of you. But she did give everything back and she's told you how sorry she is about that.' She took another hopeful glance around the room. 'Don't you think we can all forgive her now? Can we give Charlotte another chance?'

Emily gave her an enthusiastic nod. Some of the others still looked unsure, but it was a start. Relieved, Rowan went to ring the home-time bell. It had been an exhausting day.

Next morning she was watching for Clett's Jeep from her office window.

She saw him help his daughters down. Poppy skipped off, leaving her sister standing awkwardly alone, staring at the ground. Rowan saw Clett hesitate for a second, but this was something Charlotte had to do on her own. Forcing an encouraging smile, he got back in the Jeep and turned to give her a final wave as he drove slowly away.

For a long moment the little girl looked lost, then, from the other side of the playground, Rowan saw Hannah approach. The girls' conversation was brief and neither of them looked comfortable. Then Hannah pointed to the group she'd just left and Charlotte gave a reluctant nod as she followed her across the playground.

Some of the others joined them, and as they chatted Rowan could see Charlotte's little body relax. In a matter of moments she had gone from being the outsider to the centre of attention, and to Rowan's relief she looked as though she was actually enjoying it. The little face that had always appeared so sad was now smiling.

At going-home time Rowan kept a special eye out for Clett, and her heart leaped at the smile on his face as he greeted his two daughters. He strode across the playground as Rowan turned to go back into the building.

'I just wanted to say thank you. I don't know what you did but Charlotte looks like a different girl.'

Rowan smiled, nodding her agreement as she glanced across at the bobbing heads in the back of the Jeep.

'I think she's turned a corner today. She's certainly looking much happier, isn't she?'

His eyes held hers.

'I can't thank you enough,' he said quietly.

She swallowed.

'No need for that. I'm just happy to see Charlotte smiling again.'

He turned to go, then came back.

'Actually, there is one thing more you could do, Miss Fairlie. Only if you want to, that is.'

'Yes?'

'I'm taking the girls out fishing next Saturday.' He grinned. 'I don't suppose you would join us? I'll understand if you're busy.'

Fishing! She hadn't been fishing since she was a little girl when she'd gone out in the firth on Sam Meikle's boat with her dad to catch mackerel.

'I won't be busy on Saturday, and, yes, I'd love to join the three of you. Thanks for asking me.'

There was a spring in her step as she walked briskly back into school. Twenty-four hours ago she had been fearful for Charlotte Drummond's safety. Now she had a fishing expedition to look forward to!

Mystery Tour

Rowan had been listening for the arrival of Clett and the girls, and hurried to the door at the sound of tyres on the drive. But the man coming towards her made her stifle a gasp.

'Simon!' She forced a smile to cover her surprise. 'What brings you here at this time of day?'

He spread his arms in a shrug.

'Aren't you going to invite me in?'

Rowan's glance swept the road behind him. She could see no sign of the Drummond family but they would be on their way.

'Actually, Simon, I'm expecting someone.'

His top lip curled in a sneer.

'Perhaps I should make an appointment next time.'

'Hardly necessary, but a little notice might be a good idea.'

She glanced again at the still empty gateway. She had a feeling that it wouldn't be a good idea if the two men were to meet on her doorstep.

'Can I ring you later?'

He fixed her with a cold stare. No doubt he felt any other woman would have been happy to see him, excited, even. But Rowan just wanted rid of him.

He forced a smile.

'You're right. I had no right turning up unannounced, expecting you to be available for a run up north and lunch at a great lochside hotel.'

He leaned forward and his lips brushed her cheek.

'Enjoy whatever it is you have planned,' he said, a cynical smile playing on his lips. 'You don't know what you'll be missing.'

To Rowan's annoyance her efforts had been in vain. She could already see Clett's Jeep turning in at the gate. She squeezed her eyes tight shut. This wasn't supposed to happen.

Simon spun round, starting at the newcomers. Rowan could see the muscles in his neck working, but he said nothing, marching to his four-by-four and swinging himself into the driver's sear. The vehicles crawled past each other and then she heaved a sigh of relief as she saw Simon disappear down the hill.

A few seconds later Clett was out of the vehicle and standing at her door.

'Your carriage awaits, madam.' He made an exaggerated flourish. His smile was engaging.

Charlotte and Poppy were bobbing about in the back seat, their faces flushed with excitement as they set off. Sitting next to him, watching the familiar fields flying past, she said, 'Well, are you going to tell me where we're going, or is this a magical mystery tour?'

Clett gave her a smug smile but said nothing. In the back seat the girls were giggling.

'I only meant I could suggest a few

good fishing sites around here. My dad used to take me fishing,' she explained. 'There's a place just further round the shore where we used to keep a boat.' She smiled as she remembered how their battered old bicycles bounced over the tussocks of turf and heather on the track that led to the firth-side mooring. Both fishing rods would be strapped to her father's back, and the big canvas satchel, to hold the fat trout they would catch, tied securely to the back of his saddle.

Sometimes they would wait for the wind to pick up.

'Too still for fish,' her father would say.

Clett's voice broke into her thoughts.

'I thought we might go where you haven't fished before.' He smiled.

Rowan twisted round to the girls.

'I suppose you two know where we're going?'

Poppy nodded enthusiastically, and her copper curls bobbed over her eyes.

'Can we tell her, Daddy?' she

pleaded. 'Can we tell Miss Fairlie we're going to Skye?'

Charlotte gave her a push.

'You've spoiled the secret now!'

Rowan's mouth dropped open as she turned to Clett.

'Are we really going to Skye?'

He nodded.

'That's wonderful! Skye is one of my favourite places.'

The girls burst into a chorus of squeals and clapped their hands.

'We're going to Skye,' they sang in unison.

It was almost eleven o'clock when they arrived in Kyle of Lochalsh. Clett found a parking place by the harbour and they all headed for the big white hotel with a view of the bridge. Rowan and the girls clambered on to seats around a wooden table outside the hotel while Clett went inside to order drinks. He emerged minutes later with a tray laden with a silver coffee pot, jug of hot milk, cups and saucers and two glasses of juice.

To their right they could see the elegant span of the bridge. Rowan took a luxuriously deep breath, feeling the fresh air fill her lungs. Across the water, the hills of Skye looked so close she felt that if she reached forward far enough she could almost touch them.

'Glorious, isn't it?'

Rowan nodded.

'When are we crossing the bridge, Daddy? Can we go now?' Poppy whooped impatiently, brushing shortbread crumbs from her cheeks.

'I don't see why not.' He headed for the car.

As they sped across the bridge, the sparkling waters of Loch Alsh glistened through the white bars of the safety barriers. They drove on, pausing to watch a pod of whales frolicking in the water off Broadford. Then they all got out to look at the view. They could see the jagged peaks of the Cuillin Hills in the distance.

Clett breathed in the sea air and looked around him.

'I always loved coming to Skye. It's all so beautiful.' He smiled teasingly. 'How else did you think I would know such a great fishing spot?'

'I'd no idea we were in the company of such a seasoned traveller.'

Charlotte and Poppy stifled giggles.

Clett grinned.

'I wouldn't exactly say that, but I do know this little loch. You'll love it.' He ushered them all back into the vehicle.

'Is it like the loch near Balcreggan, Daddy?' Poppy piped up in the back.

'No, nothing like that. You'll see.'

It was lunchtime when they turned off what passes for a main road on the island and negotiated the winding single track that led to the fishing loch.

'Won't we need permits?'

'All sorted.' He produced a slip of folded paper from the breast pocket of his shirt and waved it at them.

Charlotte looked around her.

'There's nowhere here for lunch, and I'm starving!'

'Me, too, Daddy. I'm hungry,' Poppy echoed.

Clett got out of the vehicle and went round the back, extricating a wicker picnic basket from the boot.

'I got Mrs Moncrief to pack some food. You didn't think I was going to let us starve, did you?'

Knowing Annie Moncrief, Rowan thought, the basket would be packed with delicious goodies. She was right. Tucked beneath the red checked cloth were plastic boxes of chicken sandwiches, a bowl of green salad with baby tomatoes and an enormous crusty, home-made sausage roll. There was a carton of the girls' favourite juice and a bottle of low-alcohol Chardonnay for Clett and herself. Last of all came freshly baked apple pie.

Clett appeared behind them, his arms full of fishing rods.

'Mrs Moncrief thinks of everything. She's a treasure.'

Rowan couldn't dispute that. And later, as she watched Charlotte tucking into the picnic with obvious relish, she marvelled at the change in the little girl. Only days before the child had been distraught and miserable but there was no sign of the old Charlotte today.

She'd been deep in thought, but when she looked up she found Clett had been watching her.

'I'll be surprised if we don't pull out a few fat trout today.' He smiled.

A pair of white Sea Eagles appeared from over the far ridge and Rowan stood up and joined the girls by the waterside. They watched as one bird swooped low before turning to soar again, circling his partner. The second bird copied the manoeuvre, showing a flash of white tail feathers as it turned.

'They're dancing!' Poppy cried.

'What about this fishing?' Clett called to Rowan, sorting out the rods and tackle.

'I'll clear up these things, then sit and cheer you on.'

'Cheer us on?' Clett repeated. 'You don't imagine you are here to make up the numbers?' He thrust a fishing-rod into her hands. 'You look like a girl who knows a thing or two about fishing.'

'I used to.' Rowan laughed. 'But it's been some time since I had a rod in my hand.'

Clett shook his head.

'It's like cycling. It all comes back when you get into the saddle.'

He was right. It felt good to be in control of a fishing-rod again. She flexed her wrist and watched the line snake out across the water.

She and Clett took it in turns to guide the girls through the moves of casting. It was a surprise to all of them when Charlotte reeled in the first trout of the day. With Clett behind her, his guiding hand over his daughter's, they played the fish. Rowan rushed forward with the net as they landed it, and all four collapsed with laughter on to the soft turf of the lochside. As they struggled free, just for an instant she caught Clett's glance. The look in his eyes sent her heart pounding.

She jumped up, brushing the grass from her jeans. Clett was still watching her. Catching sight of the picnic basket she hurried over to it.

'I should tidy this lot up.'

Charlotte and Poppy had picked up their rods again and were back by the side of the loch. When she looked round she saw Clett had joined them. The moment had passed, but Rowan's heart was still pounding.

They caught four more fish that afternoon; three of them down to Clett and one to her. But when she saw the look of disappointment on Poppy's face at not having caught a fish herself, Rowan insisted on her having hers.

'It's not the same as catching it myself.' Poppy pouted.

Rowan gave her shoulders a squeeze.

'You should have more practice.' She looked across to Clett. 'Maybe Daddy can take you both on more fishing trips. There are plenty of good spots around Balcreggan.'

'Will you show them to us, Miss

Fairlie?' Rowan realised they were all looking at her. She could feel her cheeks colouring under Clett's steady gaze. This trip to Skye was one thing, but she was the children's teacher, and it wouldn't do to be seen showing them any special attention. The parents of her other pupils might consider it favouritism. No, she would have to be firm.

'I'm sure your father can find all these places for you.'

Three pairs of eyes stared, then Clett cleared his throat.

'Miss Fairlie's right. We can find all these places for ourselves. Besides, it will be fun to do a bit of exploring.'

'Would you take us exploring, Daddy?' they asked.

Clett's grimace cracked in to a smile. 'Why not?'

No sounds came from the back seat as they recrossed the bridge on their way home. Both girls were asleep.

'It's all that fresh air.' Clett gestured at them. 'They've enjoyed themselves today.'

'They loved being out with their father.'

She thought she saw him flinch.

'You're right, of course. I don't spend nearly enough time with them.'

'You're a busy man, Clett. Charlotte and Poppy understand that.'

As she spoke she wondered if she was making excuses. These little girls needed their father more than ever now.

'Busy,' he mused. 'I'm busy, all right. But it's all for them. Everything I do is to give them a secure future.' He shook his head. 'Besides, I'm not their mother. I can't do the things she did with them.'

Rowan stared.

'You think that matters? Charlotte and Poppy had a wonderful time today, and you can all do it again any time you want.' She glanced into the back to make sure the girls were still sleeping. 'It's you they want, Clett.'

He was quiet for the rest of the journey and Rowan worried that she'd spoken out of turn. But as he pulled up outside the schoolhouse, he got out to help her down. Even through the thickness of her suede jacket she could feel the heat from his hands burning through her. In the back of the vehicle the girls were beginning to stir, but he still held her.

'Thank you for today, Rowan,' he said quietly, the sincerity in his eyes once again making her heart flip over. 'I think this has been a kind of turning point for us — a new beginning. Thank you.'

An Apology

After the awkwardness of their parting yesterday Rowan flinched when she noticed that Simon was already in church when she and Evelyn arrived. They slid into the pew behind him and his mother. She remembered his annoyance when he found out she had made other plans for the day — plans that didn't include him. But she was a free agent, after all, and didn't need Simon Fraser's permission to live her life.

Hoping he had calmed down, she leaned forward and tapped him on the shoulder, giving him her widest smile when he turned.

'Rowan!' His pleasure at seeing her was genuine, but lasted only a split second. 'And Mrs Fairlie.' He nodded to Evelyn. 'How are you both this morning?'

The greeting was stiff and formal. No, Simon had obviously not forgotten yesterday's encounter.

The organ music soared, announcing the arrival of the minister. During the service Rowan glanced behind her a couple of times for any sign of Clett and the girls, but didn't spot them. She was aware of the minister's voice as he gave his sermon, but her mind was still amongst the hills and lochs of Skye, her eyes shining as she remembered the change in the two little Drummond girls.

It was a good feeling to have been part of it. But that was all she had been, she had to remind herself. She was Charlotte and Poppy's teacher, and their father had simply been grateful to her for joining them yesterday.

She hadn't realised the congregation had got to its feet to sing the final hymn until she felt a sharp nudge in her side and winced.

'Stand up, Rowan,' her mother hissed. 'I don't know what's wrong with you today!'

'Sorry,' Rowan whispered, and stood up to join in the singing.

She tried to avoid looking at Simon's back and the rigid stiffness she sensed across his broad shoulders.

The four of them emerged from the church at the same time and Evelyn moved to thank the minister for his 'thoughtful and inspiring sermon'. Rowan nodded her agreement, although she had not heard a word of it.

Simon was watching her, and the question she was dreading came when they had reached the church gate.

'I take it you had a good day yesterday?'

Rowan avoided her mother's eyes. She squared her shoulders and faced him with a determined smile.

'I did, actually.'

'Go anywhere nice?' His look was still hostile.

'We went to Skye — fishing.'

'You didn't tell me you'd gone,' Evelyn said.

Rowan shrugged.

'Mr Drummond was taking his daughters for a day out and they wanted a fourth person to make up the numbers.'

Evelyn looked at her daughter, whose expression told her not to pursue the discussion any further, not here at any rate.

Simon turned to Rowan, his eyes twinkling as though the previous conversation had never taken place.

'Any chance of us catching up later, Rowan?'

That was typical of Simon. He would plant a bomb then walk away to enjoy the ensuing explosion from a distance. Well, this time she would call his bluff.

'Why don't you call round at the schoolhouse later? I should be back there by five.' She forced a smile into her voice.

'That would be perfect,' he said, steering his mother in the direction of their car.

Rowan grimaced at their departing backs. Evelyn took her arm and began marching her to the cottage where Sunday lunch awaited them.

'You have some talking to do, young lady.' But she waited until they had eaten before returning to the subject.

Rowan laid her cutlery across her empty plate and sank back into her chair.

'That was great, Mum.' She patted her full stomach.

Evelyn flapped a hand of dismissal at her daughter.

'Never mind all that. What's this about going to Skye with the Drummonds?'

The memory brought an involuntary smile to Rowan's face. She cleared the table as she recounted the events of the previous day.

'We saw whales off Broadford and caught four fat trout at some secret loch Clett knew about. And Annie Moncrief provided the most delicious picnic lunch ever!'

'Did she now?' Evelyn hoped Rowan knew what she could be getting herself into. Clett Drummond was a widower with two little daughters to raise. But maybe she was getting ahead of herself — maybe she had misread that light in her daughter's eyes.

'So this was just a chummy kind of day out?'

Rowan nodded, a little too vigorously, Evelyn thought.

'Exactly, Mum.'

'Then why was Simon looking so jealous?'

'Was he?'

'You know very well he was.'

'Simon has no reason to be jealous.' A trace of defiance had crept into Rowan's voice. 'There's no question of any kind of romantic involvement between Clett Drummond and me. And if there were, it would still have nothing to do with Simon. He and I are just friends.'

'I don't think Simon sees it that way.'

Rowan knew her mother was right. Simon was a bad loser. But she had given him no reason to believe they would ever be a couple. Besides, it was pretty certain that Clett Drummond saw her as only his daughter's teacher. Well, that was fine. She neither wanted nor expected anything more. The stupid fluttering feeling that swept through her whenever Clett's green eyes met hers was something she would have to work out later.

* ★ ★

It was just after five when Simon's car turned into the schoolhouse drive. Rowan had been steeling herself for the meeting. There would be no raised voices. No row. She would keep her temper even if Simon lost his.

She wondered why for some reason she was drawn to him. It sometimes felt that she was the only person in the village, apart from his mother, of course, who actually did like Simon. She couldn't just abandon him. But the time had come to establish a few rules.

He arrived with a huge bunch of red roses. She couldn't imagine where he'd got such a thing on a wet Highland Sunday in March, but she smiled and accepted the gift with pleasure.

'Drink?'

He nodded and Rowan disappeared into her tiny kitchen to put the flowers in a vase and collect a bottle of wine from the fridge. She returned with the Chardonnay and two stemmed glasses.

She watched as he filled their glasses, then sat opposite him, taking a deep breath. But Simon's hand went up to silence her.

'Before you say anything, Rowan, I want to apologise for my behaviour. It was rude and childish.' He threw her a contrite glance. 'And unforgivable.'

Rowan was taken aback. Where was the usual bravado? But he hadn't finished.

'You're a lovely girl, Rowan, and you know how much I . . . admire you.' He cleared his throat. 'I don't want to lose your friendship.' He looked at her and his eyes were appealing. 'Can we start again?'

Rowan had been prepared for anger, even accusations, but not this calm reasoning. This was a new Simon, and his sentiments touched her.

She reached across the table for his hand.

'Of course we are still friends. I haven't forgotten all those great times we've had together, or how generous you've been over the past year to the school.'

She shouldn't have said that. It made it sound as though she had befriended him out of gratitude, when that wasn't the case. Still, she had to make her position clear.

'You know how highly I regard you, Simon. But I can't be more than a friend. I can't feel the way I suspect you want me to.' She sat back waiting for the reaction.

But he only smiled.

'I understand that. And I accept it.'

'You have no problem with me going out with other people?'

'So long as 'other people' isn't Clett

Drummond.' His eyes were stormy. 'That man is bad news, Rowan! You don't know him. I just want to protect you.'

'Protect me from what, for goodness' sake?' She could hear her voice rising. 'How often do I have to say it? There is nothing going on between Mr Drummond and myself. But I teach his children, Simon, so if there is something I need to know then you should tell me!'

Simon reached for the wine to replenish his glass.

'There's nothing,' he muttered. 'I just sense the man is trouble.'

By the time Simon had left, Rowan was feeling more confused than ever. Despite what he said, it was clear that he and Clett had some kind of history. But neither man seemed prepared to divulge what that was.

Next morning as she watched the children file into the school playground she tried not to look out for Clett's Jeep. It was two days now since the

Skye trip. Would everything now be back to square one?

She missed seeing the green Jeep slow to a stop in the road on the other side of the low school wall, and the first she knew of the Drummond family's arrival was when both girls bounded through the gate, tossing a backward wave to their father as they ran to join their friends.

Rowan smiled. She needn't have worried about them after all. She looked back to the gate and saw Clett standing there. He waved, and her heart gave an alarming lurch. She took a deep breath to steady herself. She had to get a grip of her feelings or they would run away with her.

Turning away she forced herself to concentrate on the day's routines, and didn't hear her sister's approach. Shona came up behind her and Rowan started when she heard her name called.

'Are you remembering tonight's meeting? It's at my place.' Shona gave her sister a quizzical look.

Rowan whirled round.

'Meeting? What meeting?'

'See? I knew you'd forgotten. The Ceilidh Committee meeting, of course. The dance is a week on Friday.'

Rowan's hand went to her temple. The annual school dance was Balcreggan Primary's biggest and most successful fund-raising event. She hadn't exactly forgotten about it — the date was in her diary and circled on the calendar in her office together with the meetings of the organising committee. But somehow she had let it slip her mind. What was happening to her?

'Of course I hadn't forgotten. Remind me again what time we are all meeting.'

'It will be just the five of us — Mum, Annie Moncrief, Dolly and us. The usual suspects.'

Rowan managed a smile.

'I'll be there, don't worry.' She shooed her sister off. 'I have one or two things to do first . . . like run a school!'

A New Arrival

Rowan was last to arrive at Shona's that evening. The four women were gathered in Shona's sitting-room, where a log-burning stove was throwing out a cosy heat. They all looked up and smiled as Rowan came in.

'Now we can get started,' Shona said, teasing.

Rowan produced the checklist she had made out.

'Shall we start with the food, then?' She looked across at Clett Drummond's housekeeper. 'You're organising the cold cuts, Annie. Is there anything you need?'

Annie shook her head.

'Mr Drummond has given permission for me to roast the gammon and beef joints in his Aga. I'll take them down to the butcher's the day before, to get them sliced. I've drafted in some helpers to put the salads together, so that's all in order, too.'

'The canapes and dips are sorted.' Evelyn smiled.

'Brilliant.'

Rowan turned to Dolly.

'The gateaux and trifles?'

'I made a batch of sponges this weekend, and they're in the freezer.' Dolly mock-scowled at Rowan. 'I have done this once or twice before, you know.'

'And it couldn't be in better hands. You don't really need me at all, do you?'

'Yes, we do,' Shona said. 'You're our publicity girl.'

'And chief ticket-seller,' Dolly cut in.

'How are the ticket sales going?' Annie asked.

Rowan smiled.

'Practically sold out.'

'Has Mr Drummond bought a ticket?' Evelyn was asking Annie but watching her daughter.

'He's intending to. I was telling him

the tickets were going fast and he said he would pick up a couple this week.'

'A couple?' Dolly's eyes sparkled with interest. 'Who is he planning on bringing with him, I wonder.'

Rowan's mother's eyes were still on her.

'His sister-in-law, I should think,' Annie replied. 'She's coming for a visit.'

Four faces lifted in unison to stare at Annie.

'Sister-in-law?' Dolly prompted, eager for more of this juicy piece of news.

Annie shrugged.

'All I know is that her name's Deena, and that she's to stay in the spare room.'

'Long-standing arrangement was it?' Dolly's wide-eyed innocence urged for more information.

'It was a last-minute thing, as far as I know. Mr Drummond rang her last night and she agreed straight away to come up.'

Shona's eyebrow lifted a fraction.

'Just like that?'

'I think they are a close family.'

Rowan stifled the urge to ask how old this Deena was. She already had a picture in her head. The old-fashioned name and the ability to rearrange her life at the drop of a hat both hinted at an older woman, a spinster who would be devoted to her two nieces.

'That's good,' she said without thinking. 'Those little girls need a woman's influence.'

Annie Moncrief straightened her back and her chin went up in a defensive tilt.

'I do what I can.' She sniffed. 'I can't run the house and play mother as well.'

'Of course you do, Annie.' Rowan reached forward to touch the older woman's arm. 'I didn't for a minute mean to suggest that it was your responsibility to look after the girls. Everybody knows you've got your hands full running the house. The Drummonds are lucky to have you.'

She saw Annie's face relax.

'That's as maybe.'

'When is this lady arriving?' Evelyn asked her.

'At the weekend, I believe.'

The conversation returned to the catering arrangements.

But Rowan knew all five of them were bursting to know more about the Drummond visitor.

All the rest of that week Clett brought the girls to school and collected them, but he never did more than nod in her direction.

Perhaps she had served her purpose in helping him with his relationship with his daughters, and now this new Auntie Deena was coming.

Rowan tried to be positive. The influence of a kindly old aunt was exactly what they needed.

Charlotte and Poppy's were looking forward to the new arrival, as was seen on Friday morning.

'Auntie Dee's coming today!' Poppy jumped up and down, clapping her hands. 'She's coming to stay and look after us. We can't wait!'

So old Auntie Dee was already working her magic — and her not even set foot in Balcreggan yet!

★ ★ ★

It had been a week since the arrival of the girls' aunt and Rowan still hadn't set eyes on her. Once she spotted a fair head and the top of a pair of glasses as the woman waited on the other side of the school wall. She would have liked to have gone up and introduced herself, but the chance never arose, for the girls scrambled into the back of Auntie Deena's black car and were whisked away.

Rowan had been trying to pace herself on the Friday of the Ceilidh. She knew the evening might be stressful, especially when she was responsible for its organisation.

She could hear the annoyance in Simon's voice when she refused his offer to collect her. But at least he'd rung first and not just turned up on her doorstep.

Perhaps he was listening to her after all.

'I have to get there early,' she told him. 'I've promised to help set up the buffet table.'

'You don't have to do that. There will be plenty of people down at the hotel lending a hand.'

'The hotel isn't doing the catering. It'll be people who give their time and effort to support the school.'

'I support the school, too!' he snapped.

That was true, even if his contribution had all been financial.

'I'm sure Balcreggan appreciates your effort, Simon.' Rowan's voice was icy.

There was an awkward pause.

'I'll see you at the dance, then.' Simon eventually said.

'I'll look forward to it.' She kept her voice light.

Rowan climbed the stairs, opened her wardrobe and ran a hand over the hanging garments. There hadn't been time to shop for something new, let alone visit the hairdresser's. She looked down at her grey skirt and matching blouse. It was smart enough, if boring. Most of the clothes in her wardrobe had that same, safe look.

Her hand lingered on a green silky print dress she'd bought on a whim last summer from a boutique in Inverness. She had never worn the dress. She lifted it out and held in front of her. She would have to sweep her hair up, but it might not look too bad, she decided.

It was two hours later when she walked into the hotel's function room. The dress fluttered around her body like a butterfly as she moved. She could feel the tendrils of hair brushing the nape of her neck, and hoped the rest of the Grecian-styled topknot didn't tumble to join them before the end of the evening.

Dolly, Annie, Shona and her mother, plus at least another six other village women, were fussing around the heavily laden buffet table. Dolly was first to look up as Rowan approached, and her eyes widened.

'You look fantastic!'

Evelyn came forward to hug her daughter.

'You'll be the belle of the ball,' she whispered.

Annie nodded her approval from behind the table and Shona called. 'You scrub up well, Sis!'

It was an hour before people started to arrive, and Rowan hurriedly pulled off the apron somebody had thrust into her hands while she helped carry more dishes from the hotel kitchen to the buffet table. The band struck up and dancers were already on the floor.

The place was filling up fast and Rowan was beginning to feel a glow of excitement. She knew Clett had bought the Crombies' two tickets, but that was no guarantee he would actually turn up.

She realised her hands were shaking. Had this been the reason she'd made such an effort with her appearance tonight. Had she been hoping to see Clett, all along?

'Rowan.' Simon appeared and took her hand, holding her at arm's length. 'You look amazing!'

He stepped back, considering her.

'There's a look about you tonight, Rowan Fairlie, that I don't think I've ever seen before.'

She coloured at the compliment.

The room was busy now, the dance floor packed with couples moving to the lilting beat of a Scottish waltz.

'Shall we?' Simon didn't wait for an answer as he drew her to him and moved into the swirl of dancers. 'A successful evening, and all down to you.'

Rowan shook her head, laughing.

'Others might have had something to do with all this.'

'But it was you who was out there leading them.'

Glancing up at him she noticed his eyes were slightly glazed. She wondered how much he'd had to drink before leaving Balcreggan House.

Suddenly, the glitter in Simon's grey eyes turned to cold steel. His stare was fixed on the door, and as Rowan turned to look her heart skipped a beat. It was Clett. He'd spotted them, too, and was returning Simon's hostile glare.

Simon made no effort to continue the dance, but was moving to the side of the floor, taking Rowan with him. She nudged his arm.

'I don't want any trouble here tonight, Simon!' she hissed.

'Tell that to your friend!' he threw back.

Clett turned his attention to Rowan and smiled across the room. Even from this distance she could see the admiration in his eyes and she felt her knees go weak. The look hadn't been lost on Simon.

She gave his arm another prod.

'Play nicely, you two, or you'll have me to answer to.'

She was trying to make light of the situation when suddenly it was taken out of her hands. Simon's eyes lit up as his gaze slid from Clett to the woman coming into the room behind him.

'I'll say this for the man, he's got taste!'

The newcomer walked towards Clett, who turned to smile at her. They made for the portable bar in the far corner. Every pair of male eyes in the room followed the tall, elegant blonde, in the red dress that clung to her body like a second skin.

'Now, who do you suppose that is?'

'I couldn't be sure,' Rowan said, her blue eyes narrowing, 'but I think that's dear old Auntie Deena.'

Rowan saw Simon's jaw begin to throb.

'Auntie? You mean she's Drummond's sister?'

Rowan shook her head.

'I got the idea she's Clett's late wife's sister.'

'I could do with a real drink. Are you coming?'

There was still anger in his voice, and

something else, too. He glanced across to the busy bar.

'Let's go through to the hotel bar.'

Rowan looked around, uncertain.'

'I shouldn't really leave the room. I'm supposed to circulate.'

'Please yourself. You know where to find me . . . if you're interested.' He strode off, leaving Rowan staring after him, mouth open.

Dolly strolled over.

'What's got into Simon Fraser?'

Rowan shook her head, frowning.

'I honestly don't know, and I don't care. He can stay in the bar all night. In fact, I hope he does!'

Dolly took her arm and led her to a quiet corner of the room.

'I don't suppose he's told you about the poaching,' she whispered, her mouth close to Rowan's ear.

'Poaching? No, he hasn't mentioned it. Has the estate been having problems again?'

Dolly nodded.

''And guess who he's blaming?' She

poked a finger at her chest.

Rowan's eyes widened.

'Surely not you, Dolly?'

'Well, not me exactly, but as good as! He's been accusing my Sam.' She took a breath, unable to control her anger. 'Now, I know Sam did take a rabbit or two in the old days, but not any more. He wouldn't put his job at Ballinbrae in jeopardy — not when Mr Drummond has been so good to him!'

'Wait a minute, Dolly.' Rowan put up a hand. 'What has been poached?'

'Trout. From that pond on the estate.'

Rowan remembered the pond. Long, lazy summer days when six whole weeks of summer holidays from school stretched ahead. It hadn't been poaching in those days, because the village children had old Sir Alex's blessing to sit around the banks with their rods and lines. They never caught more than a few tiddlers to put in their jam jars, but she still remembered the joy of sitting there in the sun, dangling bare feet in the cold, refreshing water. But things were different now. Rowan knew that Simon had filled the pond with trout and sold fishing permits to anglers anxious to catch them.

'Why is he blaming Sam?'

Dolly shrugged.

'He doesn't like him. Let's face it, Simon Fraser doesn't like anybody!' Her hand flew to her mouth. 'Sorry, Rowan. I forgot he was your boyfriend.'

'He's certainly not that! Particularly after his behaviour tonight.' She looked out towards the door through which Simon had so rudely stalked.

Dolly grabbed her arm.

'I don't want you fighting our battles for us, Rowan. We'll sort this, Sam and me.'

'We'll see about that.' Rowan strode off, shoulders back and chin up.

Inside the hotel's cocktail bar two men were facing each other, their faces contorted in anger.

'I know my workers. There is no way Sam Meikle poached your fish!' The veins in Clett's neck were standing out and his fists were clenched.

Simon caught sight of Rowan and his lip curled.

'The law's on my side, Drummond. Meikle has a history of poaching and I plan to make sure the coppers know all about that when I report him.'

Rowan strode across to stand beside Clett.

'Of course Sam didn't steal your fish,' she said angrily. 'And I can prove it!'

Femme Fatale

It was Saturday morning, but the thought of the day stretching ahead was giving Rowan no pleasure. Her feelings were in turmoil. Her fury at Simon's behaviour had not abated. How could he be so heartless? And as for Clett Drummond, swanking in to the ceilidh with Miss World on his arm . . . Rowan wasn't sure which of the men had fired her up most.

She was back in her usual attire of sweatshirt and jeans and was sipping a scalding mug of coffee at the kitchen table. She hadn't heard the crunch of tyres on the driveway, so a knock on the door made her start.

'Clett! What are you doing here?'

He inclined his head to one side and a lock of hair fell over his brow as he studied her. He grinned.

'So you're going to prove Sam

Meikle isn't the phantom poacher of Balcreggan?'

Rowan hadn't fully grasped the fact that he was standing here, in front of her.

She nodded dumbly.

'Do you have a plan?'

She cleared her throat. She was still holding the cup of coffee.

'Of course there's a plan.'

'Then I think I'd better hear it.' He brushed past her, not waiting to be invited in.

Clett's large frame dwarfed Rowan's small kitchen. He went to the window, and stood with his back to the sink. Behind him she could see boats bobbing at their moorings in Balcreggan Harbour. She was glad his face was in shade and those mesmerising eyes couldn't bewitch her.

'Well, I'm all ears,' he said. 'How do you plan to prove Sam's innocence?'

'You're making fun of me.' Rowan frowned.

'Quite the opposite, actually.' He

paused and looked down, crossing his legs at the ankles. 'I thought you were amazing last night, Rowan.'

The gentleness of his voice made her weak. If only her heart would stop fluttering about like a manic butterfly. She should accept the compliment graciously, but the image of him with the elegant woman by his side last night intruded.

'I assume that was your sister-in-law at the ceilidh? You never introduced us.'

He nodded.

'That's right. Deena. She's come to stay for a bit. The girls adore her.'

Did anyone else in the house 'adore' her?

'I'm sorry you weren't introduced.' He looked down, clearing his throat. 'The opportunity didn't arise. But I didn't come here to discuss Deena. I came about Sam. Seems to me we both want to help him.'

He lifted an eyebrow for confirmation and Rowan nodded.

'Well, go on,' he said, arms still

folded. 'Tell me about this plan of yours.'

'Right,' she began hesitantly, glancing past him as the *Feisty Lass*, one of Balcreggan's few remaining commercial fishing boats, chugged out of the harbour. 'It's simple. I plan to keep an all-night vigil on the pond.' She saw his mouth was beginning to curl into a grin. 'I have a camera,' she went on. 'When the culprit turns up I'll take a picture of him.'

Clett's green eyes were studying her again.

'As simple as that?'

She began tidying away the coffee things nervously.

'I didn't say it was a great plan, but tell me, have you any better ideas?'

She turned round and their eyes met. For a few seconds no-one spoke.

'Maybe I do,' he replied. 'How about if I come with you on that all night vigil?'

Rowan stared at him.

'You want to come with me?'

'You don't think I would let you do this on your own, do you? Besides, I have night glasses, and a top-of-the-range camera.'

'Why would you want to do that?'

'I have a stake in this too, remember. I don't believe any more than you do that Sam is guilty. It's just another one of Simon Fraser's tricks.'

'You talk as if you know Simon quite well.'

'I know he's a snake! And I'm pleased you have found him out at last.' He was frowning at her. 'Haven't you?'

She sighed.

'I thought he was kind and generous . . . at first. He seemed so keen to support the school.'

'Maybe he was trying to get into your good books.'

Rowan bit her lip.

'Perhaps,' she said reluctantly. 'Everyone warned me about him, but I didn't see it. I thought he was just being possessive whenever he expected me to fall in with his plans. But I saw him in a different light last night.' She stole a look at him. 'He doesn't like you very much, Clett. Does he?'

He shrugged.

'The feeling's mutual.'

'I find that hard to believe, Clett.' Her hand went out in an involuntary gesture and touched his arm. 'I don't see you as a man who would harbour hatred for anyone.'

She heard his sharp intake of breath.

'That's because you don't really know Simon.'

There was a chilling edge to his voice, and she was relieved when he said no more. There would come a time when she would ask Clett exactly what Simon had done to him, but that time wasn't now.

When he left, Rowan went back to her window, but this time the view was no distraction. She couldn't believe she'd just agreed to spend the night with Clett, hiding in the bushes by a cold and damp fish pond as they waited to trap an unsuspecting poacher.

She wondered what Auntie Deena would make of it if he told her, but somehow Rowan guessed he wouldn't.

★ ★ ★

Usually, her routine was to collect her mother and head off to the supermarket in the nearby town of Invermore, but her head was buzzing from Clett's visit. She drove through the village, parking at Evelyn's cottage.

'Is that you, Rowan? I'm not quite ready,' her mother called out as Rowan let herself in the back door.

'Don't worry, Mum. I'll take a stroll down to the harbour and be back in half an hour or so.'

Grey clouds were on the horizon on the other side of the firth. She prayed it wouldn't rain tonight. Crouching amongst the trees by the edge of Simon's pond would be uncomfortable enough without having to deal with a downpour as well! But at least she would have Clett for company.

She wandered along the waterfront. Balcreggan had once been a thriving fishing port, providing a living for the local families. Nowadays, with the exception of the *Feisty Lass*, most of the boats in the harbour were purely for their owners' leisure pursuits.

She was so deep in thought that she didn't see the little Drummond girls jumping up and down in excitement at the end of the quay.

'Miss Fairlie!' Charlotte yelled, and Poppy waved.

The woman with them watched as Rowan approached. There was no trace of last night's femme fatale image. This morning Deena Traquair was quite the countrywoman. Her dark jeans had been zipped into what Rowan suspected were very expensive brown leather boots. Her short sheepskin jacket covered a white polo-neck sweater and her flowing blonde hair was held with an Alice band.

She put out her hand.

'We didn't meet last night. I'm Dee

Traquair.' She smiled fondly at the girls. 'Charlotte and Poppy's aunt.'

Rowan took her hand. The grip was firm.

'Rowan Fairlie.' She smiled politely. 'How long are you staying?' She hadn't meant to ask that outright, the words were out before she could stop them.

Dee's beautiful tawny eyes narrowed.

'For as long as I'm needed,' she said, still studying her.

Rowan fixed her attention on the girls.

'How lucky for you two, having your aunt Dee come to stay!'

Charlotte slid a hand into Dee's.

'It's brilliant,' she said quietly.

Dee hugged both her nieces.

'Brilliant for me, too!' She gave them a squeeze and looked up at Rowan, who forced a smile.

'That's wonderful. I think the girls are beginning to get used to us in Balcreggan.'

They both nodded enthusiastically.

'Miss Fairlie came with us to Skye

and Mrs Moncrief made us a picnic, and we saw whales and sea eagles dancing!' Poppy said breathlessly, holding her arms wide to demonstrate the birds' flight.

Dee gave Rowan a cold stare.

'My brother-in-law told me about Skye. He didn't mention you'd been with them.'

Rowan shrugged and tried to sound casual.

'I think I was just invited to make up the numbers.'

She wondered what Dee would think if she knew about tonight's little adventure!

'We're going down to the beach to look for creepy crawlies under the rocks!' Poppy said.

Dee's nose wrinkled in a gesture of distaste.

'I didn't say anything about creepy crawlies.'

Poppy ignored that.

'Can Miss Fairlie come with us? Please?'

'I'm sure Miss Fairlie sees quite enough of you two in school all week.' Dee looked at her.

'That's not so. I love the girls' company. We all had a great time in Skye, didn't we, girls?' She smiled at Charlotte and Poppy. 'Sadly, I do have to be somewhere else today, so I can't come down to the beach with you.

She pointed across to the other side of the pebbly beach where there was a strip of white sand.

'But if you head over in that direction you can find all kinds of shells and tiny white pebbles that you can take back home to make into pictures.'

'Will there be crabs and creepy things over there?'

Rowan turned towards her mother's cottage.

'Oh, yes.' She laughed. 'Lots of creepy things!'

'I told you Miss Fairlie knows all about beaches!' she heard Poppy call as they scrambled to the pebbly shore.

She was smiling as she went into her

mother's kitchen.

'Well, it's nice to see you smiling. We all thought you were going to kill somebody last night!'

'Simon? You're right. I could have killed him.'

Evelyn nodded.

'Along with practically everybody else at the dance. Imagine accusing Sam Meikle of poaching! Dolly was livid. If you want my opinion, Simon Fraser was just out to cause trouble last night.' She frowned. 'What got into him?'

Rowan didn't know, only that it involved Clett Drummond, and poor Sam had somehow got caught in the middle. Maybe she could persuade Clett to talk about it tonight.

She felt a shiver of excitement run down her spine. What would her mother think if she knew what they were planning? She didn't really care. She was going to prove Sam's innocence, and Clett would be with her.

Many Balcreggan locals shopped at

the Invermore supermarket, so Rowan was not surprised to hear her name being called as she packed her groceries into bags at the checkout.

'I've just seen Evelyn and persuaded her to come for a cup of coffee in the café!' Annie Moncrief called down the queue. 'Will you join us?'

Rowan nodded.

'I'll be right with you, Annie, once I've loaded this lot into the boot.'

With the shopping of all three women safely locked up in their respective cars, they sat sipping large mugs of latte in the store's cafeteria.

'I needed this.' Annie put her coffee mug down and shifted on the uncomfortable plastic chair. 'I was shattered by the time I got back to Ballinbrae last night!'

The others nodded. They had all stayed behind after the ceilidh to clear up the aftermath of the buffet.

'How are you getting on with that visitor?' Evelyn reached across the table to help herself to an iced pastry. 'She wasn't what we were expecting.'

She was making an effort not to look at her daughter.

'She came as a surprise to me, too.' She gave a little cough. 'I assumed she was an older, more homely kind of woman.' She stopped. 'I don't know why I thought that, because their mother had been very glamorous, too.'

'The family must still miss her terribly,' Evelyn said. 'I know it's been a year since she was killed, but it takes time to get over something like that. If you ever do.'

Annie's brows came together in a frown.

'They'll all get over it quick enough now, if that sister has anything to do with it.' She glanced around the café to make sure she wouldn't be overheard.

'She's after him.' She sniffed. 'It's obvious.'

Rowan and her mother exchanged looks. Rowan wasn't sure they should be talking like this, but she felt compelled to listen.

'You're talking about Mr Drummond,' Evelyn said. 'In what way is she after him?'

'Well, it all kicked off last night with that Simon Fraser at the ceilidh.' She tutted. 'Ridiculous to accuse Sam Meikle of poaching! Anyway, Mr Drummond was still raging about it when he got back to the farm, calling Simon for everything under the sun.'

She leaned back.

'And there was Deena trying to pacify him with strong drink, as if that was going to help. But then I don't doubt she had her reasons for wanting to get him drunk. She's trying to get her feet under the table.' Annie tapped the side of her head. 'The woman has this high-flying job in Glasgow, but that's not enough for her.'

She paused to see the effect her words were having on Rowan and Evelyn, and then continued.

'People think Clett Drummond is just a tenant farmer, but there's more to him than that.'

Rowan held up her hand to stop any of Annie's further revelations. She didn't like Clett's private business being bandied around like this.

'I don't think we should be gossiping like this.'

Evelyn frowned at her daughter, but Annie nodded.

'Rowan's right, we mustn't gossip. I'm just worried for those two little girls.'

She bit her lip.

'I can't see Deena Traquair making a great mother to them. Oh, she's full of fun and makes it her business to spend a lot of time with them. And they like the fact that she's glamorous, like their mother was. But if that young woman does wheedle her way into Mr Drummond's affections, I doubt she'll be putting the girls first.'

'This is not our business, Annie,' Rowan protested. 'It's up to Mr Drummond. He's a grown man.'

'He's a man who needs a mother for his daughters!' Annie responded.

The conversation was still ringing in Rowan's ears as she drove her mother back to Balcreggan. Could Annie be right? She remembered the possessive way Deena had held on to her nieces' hands when she'd met them earlier at the harbour.

She was beautiful, and by all accounts she was a successful career woman. And Clett still had his company in Inverness. Deena was no doubt quite capable of running that single-handed.

Something was niggling at her, something that involved Simon and Clett. They both had businesses in Inverness. Was that how they knew each other?

But if they had known each other in Inverness, and Simon already hated Clett as much as he appeared to, then why had he leased Ballinbrae Farm to him?

Stake Out!

Rowan was back at her kitchen window, staring out to the harbour again, the bags of groceries still on the table where she'd dumped them when she got in almost an hour before.

She shook her head. What was she doing? She'd declared in front of everyone at the ceilidh that she would get the proof that Sam Meikle was not the poacher.

Now she examined her motives and began to feel ashamed of herself. She hadn't been thinking of Sam, nor Dolly. She'd only wanted to hit back at Simon. And now she had gone and got Clett involved in her hair-brained scheme.

She glanced at the clock. It was mid afternoon. There was still time to ring Clett and call the whole thing off.

Her hand, poised over her mobile

phone, was halted by a sharp rap on her door. When she went to open it she found Dolly fidgeting on the doorstep.

'I had to come. I don't know what else to do!' she rushed in and Rowan followed her into the kitchen.

'What's happened, Dolly?' she frowned, guiding her friend on to a chair.

'You said you had proof that Sam didn't do the poaching.' She was looking at Rowan with wide, pleading eyes. 'If you know who's doing this you have to tell me, Rowan. I'm going mad here!'

Rowan bit her lip and pulled out the chair opposite Dolly.

'I didn't exactly say I knew who was doing it,' she began, hesitantly.

She was wishing more than ever that she hadn't started this. Why couldn't she hold her tongue?

Dolly stared at her.

'You mean you don't know? But you said . . . '

Rowan reached for her friend's hand.

'I don't know for sure, but I've

thought of a way to find out.'

Dolly looked up sharply.

'What way? If you know anything you must tell me now!'

Rowan lowered her voice, speaking in a softer tone.

'Nobody believes Sam's guilty.'

'Simon Fraser does.' Dolly spoke bitterly then released a long painful sigh. 'Oh, Rowan, you don't know what this is doing to my Sam! We thought all this kind of thing was behind us.

'A few rabbits, a couple of salmon . . . that's all he ever took, and old Sir Alex never seemed to mind. But this man, Fraser, he's out to get us. He won't rest until he sees Sam sacked.' She was on the verge of tears. 'He loves his job up at Ballinbrae. He can't lose it, Rowan, not for something he didn't do!'

Any thoughts Rowan had had of pulling out of the night's escapade were now gone. There was no way she wouldn't do her best to help her friends. She squeezed Dolly's hand.

'Clett will not sack Sam, not over this. He knows what Simon is like. Go home, Dolly. Leave this to me.'

She watched Dolly slowly cross the deserted playground and go through the school gate.

I've done it again, she thought. Committed myself to something that at best was only giving the people she cared about false hope.

What chance was there of her and Clett catching a poacher? She had a sudden horrible thought. What if there was a gang of them?

What had she let them in for?

She made herself a light supper and tried not to watch the clock. Clett was a man of his word. He'd said nine, and that was when he would turn up.

But as the hands of the clock crept on, the old doubts began to flood in. It was a crazy idea. She should call Clett and cancel the thing.

Instead, she went to the cupboard and brought out her flask, filled it with hot coffee and made a round of ham sandwiches. She packed them, together with her digital camera, into the small rucksack she often took with her on the solitary lochside walks she enjoyed, and hung it over a kitchen chair.

She was guessing Clett wouldn't be late, but she still jumped when he knocked the door.

She opened it and nodded a greeting, following him back into the kitchen.

'We've time for a coffee,' she said, 'if you want to.'

He shook his head.

'I've been thinking.'

His eyes followed her as she fidgeted around the cupboard where the china was stored.

'There's no need for you to come, Rowan. In fact, I don't think you should.' He hesitated, his green eyes full of concern. 'I don't know what we might find, and it might get dangerous.'

Rowan banged the cupboard door closed.

'All the more reason for us to go together. It was my idea, remember.'

She was jabbing a finger at her chest. 'Sam and Dolly are my friends . . . and besides, you don't know where the pond is.'

Clett was shaking his head at her, but there was a twinkle of amusement in his eyes. He put his hands up.

'OK, you win. It's your show.' He wagged a finger. 'But remember, no heroics. No matter what we find, we just sit back and watch, and take pictures.'

'Of course,' she said, nodding with a sly smile.

* * *

'We won't be needing the Jeep,' she told him as they left the schoolhouse. 'We can skirt the edge of the golf course and climb over a wall into the estate.'

Clett had brought his own small rucksack and hoisted it over his shoulder as he looked down at her.

'You've done this before!' He grinned accusingly.

She pointed into the darkness.

'It's that way.'

The going was rough and they stubbed their toes in a few rabbit holes before reaching the low stone wall that bordered the Balcreggan Estate. Rowan scrambled ahead of him through the trees.

He touched her shoulder.

'Are you sure you know where you're going?'

'It's just along here,' Rowan whispered, nodding ahead. 'This is the pond.'

Clett came up beside her. The moon had come out again from a gap in the clouds and was illuminating the water like some ethereal floodlights at a football game.

'It's not very big,' he said, scanning it. 'Half an acre at most, I'd say.'

Rowan nodded, discarding her rucksack on to the ground.

'We can probably just see all the edges from here. I think we should watch from here.'

Clett eased off his own rucksack and produced a rubber sheet, which he spread on the ground. He saw her surprised look.

'Well, I wasn't prepared to catch pneumonia!'

'I'm impressed.' She dropped to her knees.

He tapped his rucksack.

'Night goggles, camera, I've come prepared.'

Rowan copied his gesture.

'Flask, sandwiches . . . so have I!'

The moon had retreated to behind its cloud again but their eyes were getting used to the darkness.

'How do you know this place?'

'We used to come here when I was little. It was like an adventure playground to the village children. In those days the estate was owned by a lovely old man called Sir Alexander Gifford-Bane. He never minded us playing here, so long as we didn't damage anything, and of, course we never did.'

She sighed, remembering.

'Actually, I had special privileges. My father was the estate manager here before he died, so there's not much I don't know about this place. But it was special to all of us in Balcreggan. I think Sir Alex saw the estate as belonging to the village, and not the other way round.'

'Pity his successor doesn't see it that way.' He'd propped himself up on his elbow to look at her. 'What are you doing with a man like that, Rowan?'

She paused before speaking.

'If you're talking about Simon, I'm not exactly with him, as you put it. I never have been, not in any romantic way. Oh, I don't know. He hasn't won over the locals since he and his mother have been here.' She shrugged. 'I suppose I just took pity on him because he seemed so vulnerable.'

'Vulnerable? Simon Fraser is about as vulnerable as an adder!'

Rowan's sigh was heartfelt.

'I'm beginning to see that. I couldn't believe he would accuse Sam of poaching — and in front of everyone. His behaviour was disgraceful! I've never seen him act like that before. Oh, I know he can be difficult. I suppose I always gave him the benefit of the doubt. It can't be easy running an estate like Balcreggan as well as his property business.'

She twisted round to look at him.

'You know about Simon's other business, don't you?' She could only see the outline of his face, but she knew his expression was grim.

He said nothing so she went on.

'It's based in Inverness, but he has offices all over Scotland.' A sudden thought struck her. 'Your construction company is in Inverness. Is that how you two know each other?'

He nodded.

'We met there, yes.' An icy coldness had crept into his voice. 'I'm more interested in what you see in the man.'

'I don't see anything in him, not any more.'

She thought back to the first time she

set eyes on Simon. He'd been with his mother in church that day. The fact that he was so attentive to the old woman had impressed Rowan.

'He was very kind when we first met. He told me he was interested in my work at the school and said he wanted to do his bit for the community by providing new gymnastic equipment. He also paid for a carpenter to come in and build a portable library and filled the shelves with books.' She paused. 'He seemed like a good man.'

'Were you in love with him?' Clett asked quietly.

She stared at his face in the darkness.

'In love with him?' Rowan was horrified. 'Whatever gave you that idea? Of course I wasn't in love with him! Although he probably wanted me to be. But that was never going to happen. I just didn't think of him that way. He was a friend, good company, and I enjoyed going out with him.'

She heard Clett clear his throat and

she swallowed back the indignation that was growing inside her.

'You think I led him on?' she accused. 'But it wasn't like that. Simon knew exactly where he stood with me. I told him we could never be more than friends, and he accepted that.'

Clett took her hands, and the warmth of his touch sent an unexpected wave of excitement surging through Rowan.

'I'm glad. He would never have been good enough for you.'

There was a rustle in the undergrowth and they both froze. Clett put a finger to his lips. Rowan could feel her heart pounding as she slowly reached for her bag and slid out the camera. They sat motionless, staring into the darkness. The sound came again, closer this time. If this was the poachers, they were being careful.

As if on cue, the moon once again slid into a gap between the clouds and the pond was bathed in silvery light. Twenty yards away to their right, the undergrowth by the edge of the water began to rustle, then the trout poacher appeared!

Rowan's hand flew to her mouth as she raised the camera. The first intruder was followed by two others and they all slid stealthily into the water.

Rowan and Clett held their breaths. Moments later, the first otter reappeared above the surface of the water, followed by her two smaller offspring. Each creature had a fat, wriggling trout firmly grasped in its mouth.

Both cameras clicked, Rowan's flash going off and startling the otters into retreat. All three animals scurried off, still gripping their fish.

Clett and Rowan stared at each other then collapsed on the rubber sheet, laughing.

'Well, I think we've found Fraser's poachers.' Clett shook his head in disbelief. 'Did you know that was going to happen?'

'I have seen otters here once or twice before, but I wasn't expecting this.'

She didn't know how it happened,

but suddenly Clett had his arms around her and his lips were brushing her hair.

'I'm liking Balcreggan more and more every day,' he whispered, and kissed her.

It was the gentlest kiss she'd ever known. His lips, hesitant, shy, were the merest touch on hers. Rowan's heart was singing. Above them the sky was a velvety blue and the stars were so close that she believed she could almost reach out to touch them.

It was minutes before they drew apart, staring breathlessly at each other.

'I'm sorry, Rowan. I shouldn't have done that.'

But she touched her fingers to his lips. Surely he wasn't regretting it already!

'It was just a kiss, Clett,' she whispered. 'Just a kiss.'

She mustn't take that kiss for anything more than a reaction to the moment. For all she knew he was all set to propose to the beautiful Deena. Maybe he had even already done so.

They'd found what they were looking for. They had discovered Simon's poachers, and she had the evidence right there in her camera.

Clett reached forward to pull up the collar of Rowan's jacket and wrapped it around her neck.

'I should get you home,' he said.

They didn't speak much on the trek back to the schoolhouse. Several times Clett took her arm to steady her when she lost her footing. Rowan hoped that kiss was not going to spoil her relationship with the Drummond family. She was too fond of them all to bear that.

It was just after midnight when they reached the schoolhouse. Rowan hesitated. She couldn't let him just go off like this.

'I have some brandy. We're both chilled to the bone, and I think . . . '

She didn't get the chance to finish the sentence.

'I thought you'd never ask,' he said, grinning down at her.

Rowan went into the schoolhouse ahead of Clett and dumped her bag on the kitchen table before going through to the tiny sitting-room to turn on the gas fire. He was still in the kitchen and she nodded to a cupboard where the brandy and glasses were kept.

He poured two good measures and followed Rowan through to the fire.

They were comfortable in each other's company again, relaxed after the night's successful exploit.

'Will you tell the girls about this?'

Clett frowned.

'I'm not sure. I've no doubt they would think it was a hoot, a great adventure.' He grimaced. 'But the grown-ups might not see it that way. You and me going off into the night together, crouching in the woods waiting for a poacher!'

Rowan laughed.

'Put that way it does seem a bit far-fetched.' She met his eyes. 'Are you worried that Deena might take it the wrong way?'

'Deena? What's it got to do with her?'

Somewhere inside her a tiny glimmer of hope began to beat.

'I'm sorry; it's this village. It's full of gossips.'

Clet raised an eyebrow.

'And they're gossiping about Deena and me?' His look was incredulous. 'There's nothing going on in that direction, I can assure you. Charlotte and Poppy like the fuss she makes of them, and I was grateful when she agreed to come up here to join us, but she won't be staying.'

'Does Deena know that?' Rowan asked doubtfully. 'I rather think she might have her own agenda.'

Clett swirled the remains of his brandy around his glass and shook his head.

'Never in a million years.'

'I'm sorry, Clett, I should never have said that. I know how much you must still be grieving for your wife.'

It was a long time before he spoke.

'I'm not grieving for Rachel,' he said.

'It breaks my heart that Charlotte and Poppy still miss her so much, but our marriage was over long before the accident.'

He sat forward, gazing into the fire, his eyes seeing back into the past.

'I was still building the company in Glasgow when I met Rachel. It must be ten years ago now. She was secretary to a business acquaintance. We got on straight away. Everything was great at first, even though we didn't have much money. We worked well together, then the girls came along and I thought our life was perfect.'

He pursed his lips, his eyes still on the fire.

'I suppose you could say success ruined our marriage. Rachel couldn't spend our money fast enough. Everything had to be the best, furniture, clothes, cars, and holidays. Charlotte and Poppy were becoming totally spoiled. Rachel insisted on them going to a private school where it seemed to me all the teachers looked near retirement age. That didn't matter to her, though, because the school had the right name, the right image.

'She became obsessed with the high life. People I hardly knew were invited to our home for cocktail parties and lavish dinners. It didn't seem to matter whether I was there or not.'

He took a shaky breath.

'Her affairs were the last straw. She didn't even bother to be discreet about them any more.'

Rowan stared at him, hardly able to believe what she was hearing. All this time she had thought Clett was broken-hearted. She'd seen the look of sadness behind his green eyes and assumed it was grief for his lost love, when all the time it was sorrow on behalf of his daughters.

'She wasn't alone that night,' he said flatly.

'The night of the accident?'

He nodded.

'There was a man with her — the

current man she was having an affair with.'

Rowan frowned, trying to remember what her mother had told her about this accident.

'Sorry, but I thought Rachel was on her own in the car. Isn't that what the newspapers said?'

'That was the conclusion of the Fatal Accident Inquiry.' He stared into the fire, his expression grim. 'But I believe otherwise. I've no proof, of course, but I won't stop searching.'

Rowan sat up, staring at him.

'What makes you think she wasn't alone in the car?'

'For a start, the driving seat was pulled back. Rachel was short, only five foot four. She always pulled the driving seat as far forward as it would go.'

He tipped up his glass and threw back the last of his brandy.

'Not only do I think she was with another man, but I also think it was him who was driving.'

The Poachers

The first thing Rowan thought of next morning when she woke up was that Clett had kissed her. She screwed her eyes tight shut again reliving every second of the exquisite moment, not willing to let one tiny part of it escape. He had kissed her, and she had kissed him back. There was a connection between them that she had hardly dared admit before but now she wanted to scream it from the rooftops.

He didn't have any feelings for Deena. He wasn't going to marry her! Rowan's heart was singing. There had been no talk of feelings between them yet she knew they were there. They both knew that.

She hugged herself, unwilling to let the moment slip away. All this, and they had proved Sam's innocence, too! How she would enjoy watching Simon's face when she showed him the pictures of the real culprits that had been helping themselves to his fish.

Reluctantly she slipped out of bed and padded through to the kitchen to retrieve her camera from the rucksack then went to her laptop to download the otter pictures. Despite the darkness they had come out well. Three startled otters gazed back at her, a trout still dangling from each of their mouths.

'Well, Simon Fraser.' She smiled to herself. 'Let's see what you have to say about this!'

★　★　★

Simon and his mother were still having breakfast when she drove up to Balcreggan House and hammered at the door, insisting on seeing him. Ignoring Maisie Gillespie's instructions to wait in the hall, she strode into the dining-room and slapped the pictures on the table in front of him.

'There are your poachers!' she

declared, pointing at the images.

Simon and Geraldine stared open-mouthed, first at her then at the pictures.

'I think you owe someone an apology.'

Simon lifted the prints and frowned at them.

'May I ask how you came by these?' he asked, curtly.

She wasn't prepared for the question.

'I . . . I went out there last night and took the pictures.'

He looked up, frowning.

'You were trespassing, then,' he said, his eyes cold.

Geraldine got to her feet; her hands out in a placatory gesture.

'Let's not get this thing out of proportion,' she reasoned. 'If these pictures are genuine . . . '

Rowan's eyes widened.

'Of course they're genuine.'

' . . . then a mistake has been made and the wrong person has been accused. I suggest that everyone just stays calm then we can sort this out.'

Simon got up and came round the table to face Rowan.

'Are you seriously telling me that you spent the night lying in wait beside my pond for these creatures?' His expression was incredulous.

Rowan nodded uneasily.

'On your own?'

This was difficult. There was no way she could involve Clett. An already fraught situation might explode if she mentioned his name.

She raised her chin defiantly and met his eyes.

'Who in their right mind would have been mad enough to join me?' she snapped. 'Do you imagine I took Dolly along with me?'

She was saying anything to distract him. If Simon discovered Clett Drummond had been on his land he might be vindictive enough to call the police. But to Rowan's amazement, Simon expression changed and he began to laugh.

'You're a woman full of surprises,

Rowan Fairlie. Come, sit down and join us for coffee.'

He pulled out a chair and beckoned to Maisie, who had been hovering at the door, to fetch a fresh pot of coffee.

As Rowan sat down, Geraldine excused herself, saying she had things to do.

'I've chased your mother away. I shouldn't have charged in like that.' She slid him a still hostile glance. 'It wasn't her who upset everyone at the ceilidh, after all.'

Simon glanced down at his half-eaten breakfast and cleared his throat.

'Was I that bad?'

She nodded.

'How can I make amends?'

'First you have to apologise publicly to Sam and Dolly. I think maybe Mr Drummond is also owed an explana-tion.'

Simon's brows came together and his hand went up.

'You're going too far there, Rowan.'

Rowan gave an exasperated sigh.

'What is it with you two? You behave as though you hate each other.' She stared at him. 'Do you want to tell me about it?'

He shrugged.

'Not much to tell. We met through an acquaintance in the property business in Inverness. He had some kind of construction company out on the industrial estate. We socialised a bit, a few dinners, that sort of thing.' He picked up the bread roll on his plate and crumbled it through his fingers. 'We had an interest in the same property.' He shrugged again. 'What can I say? I won, he lost. He's been bitter every since.'

'That's it?' Rowan was staring at him wide-eyed. She didn't believe a word of this. Clett would never be so petty. And as far as business went she sensed that he had more expertise, even if he were less ruthless than Simon.

What was so terrible that neither of them was prepared to speak of it?

The maid brought in a tray on which

were a silver coffee pot, fine blue china cup, saucer and spoon. Simon refilled his cup and poured one for Rowan.

'There's one thing I don't understand,' she pressed. 'Why lease Ballinbrae Farm to a man you dislike so much?'

Simon's mouth took on a hard line.

'I didn't know. I left the arrangements in the hands of my agent in Inverness. The client had a background in farming and wanted to move to the Highlands, they said. OK, I know I should have asked questions, but I didn't. The deal went through and the papers were signed, and the first I knew who my tenant was when Drummond marched into my office here and demanded the keys.'

Rowan shook her head, frowning.

'But Clett must have known he was dealing with you?'

His shoulders lifted in a gesture of helplessness.

'He says not. He was dealing with a company called Highland Properties. My name didn't appear . . . so he says.'

His eyes narrowed. 'I wouldn't put it past him to have instigated the whole thing, just to wind me up!'

Rowan was aghast.

'That's cruel. The man had only recently lost his wife in a horrible road accident. Getting his own back on an old adversary would be the last thing on his mind.'

Simon jumped to his feet with such force that his chair almost fell over. He went to the window and stood with his back to Rowan. She couldn't see his expression.

'Perhaps you're right.'

When he turned back he was smiling.

'I'll make a point of catching up with Meikle at lunchtime.' He gave her a sly look. 'Do you think the pub would be public enough for the apology?'

'Definitely.' Rowan stood up to go.

'Perhaps we could have lunch later?'

'I don't think so,' she said curtly. 'I don't think we'll be sharing any more social occasions, do you?'

She saw his jaw drop and she turned

on her heel and left. All in all it had been a satisfying encounter. She'd made her point about Sam and, hopefully, Simon was in no doubt that any friendship they had was now well and truly over.

But the animosity between the men was still a mystery.

Back in the car she checked her watch. The Drummond family would certainly be up and about by now — and she had good news to share. Clett would be delighted when she told him about Simon's promise to apologise to Sam.

The yard was quiet as she drove in. She could see the Jeep parked at the side of the farmhouse building. The front door was ajar, but no-one heard her knock. She went in, peeking into the kitchen as she passed. The breakfast dishes had been washed and were stacked in the drainer to dry. There was no sign of Annie Moncrief or the girls, so Rowan walked on, pausing as she reached the door to the large large sitting-room.

She could see inside. A fire was crackling in the hearth, ornaments on the mantelshelf were gleaming, and cushions had been plumped up.

But Rowan didn't notice any of this. She was rooted to the spot, her eyes wide with disbelief. Clett and Deena were locked in an apparently passionate embrace; too busy kissing each other to even notice her.

Her hand flew to her mouth and she turned to flee, her face contorted with pain. No-one followed her, they probably hadn't even realised she was there. She got quietly into her car, slid it into gear and drove out of the yard with no idea where she was going, only that she had to get away from that room and that memory, before anyone from the house saw her.

She drove blindly, hardly noticing the village slip past, and didn't give way until she was well away from the familiar cottages. She took the road that ran along the side of the loch and turned off into a small parking area used by walkers.

She left the car and strode along the side of the loch, gulping in the cold air and staring out at the black water.

She wouldn't allow Clett to do this to her. He'd let her down. He wasn't worth her tears, she decided, but they flowed anyway in an uncontrollable torrent. She swiped angrily at her wet cheeks. Why had he lied to her? Why say he had no interest in Deena, when her own eyes had shown her this was far from the truth?

She was out of the car and walking now, striding along the side of the loch, gulping in the cold air. Her mobile rang and she reached into her pocket and glanced at the screen. It was Clett, the last person she wanted to talk to. She'd been so excited as she drove up to Ballinbrae, couldn't wait to see his face when she told him about Simon's intention to apologise to his farm manager. Maybe he didn't care, maybe the whole thing was a pretence.

She ran a hand through her hair. She had always thought herself such a good judge of character, and here was this man who had completely wrong-footed her. Could she ever trust her own judgment again? Her mobile sprung into life again and she reached to cancel the call when she saw Clett's name appear. There was no way she was going to talk to him.

The breeze had stiffened and a bank of dark clouds was beginning to roll in from the north. Rowan pulled her jacket closer and shivered. Why couldn't Clett just have been honest with her? She would have understood. But when he kissed her he'd given her false hope, and that was cruel. He was just as bad as Simon.

Twice more she cancelled calls from Clett and when it rang a fifth time she felt like hurling it into the loch. But when she glanced at the screen she saw the call was from her mother. She clicked it to answer.

'Rowan, where are you? Why didn't

you call on me for church?'

Church! The world had carried on while she'd been in turmoil. She made an effort to pull herself together.

'I'm sorry, Mum, I just needed to get away from the village for an hour or so.' She stared out across the choppy water. 'I'm on the path that goes around the loch.'

Evelyn let out a gasp.

'In this weather? It must be freezing out there today — and the forecast is for snow!'

'I'm fine, Mum, honestly.'

But her mother was right. The weather did look threatening, and her thin denim jacket was no protection for this biting wind.'

'You've missed lunch,' Evelyn said. 'I could put something in the oven for you when you get back.'

'Don't go to any trouble, Mum. I'm not hungry. Anyway, I'm heading back now.'

'Has your phone been switched off, Rowan? Clett Drummond has been

215

trying to get in touch with you. He rang me asking if I knew where you were.'

Despite herself, the mere mention of his name sent her heart lurching.

'I must have missed his calls,' she lied.

'Well, he rang me, asking if I knew where you were.'

Rowan swallowed. Her mother mustn't ring Clett and tell him her whereabouts. She didn't want him turning up here, demanding why she was blocking his calls.

She tried to keep her voice light.

'I'll call him, but I'll be back home in no time.'

'If you're sure, dear. Ring me when you get home, won't you?' Her mother rang off.

Rowan slipped the phone back into her pocket. The exchange had helped to calm her. She could see things more clearly now. She was no longer blinded by rage.

Clett had merely been kind. That kiss had been a spur of the moment thing, probably down the to the circumstances they were in. She'd been at fault to read any more into it. She just had to keep telling herself that.

She turned and headed for home, the sharp wind in her back now. She'd probably faced the worst of the weather just getting to this spot — and she hadn't noticed any of it. She took time now to study the sky. The clouds didn't look quite so black and they were moving at a rate across the tops of the far hills.

Only last week, Balcreggan had been bathed in warm sunshine. Little patches of gold and purple crocuses had appeared in the borders of her tiny garden. It was spring, for heaven's sake!

The memory of her crocuses cheered her slightly. The children had planted them last September. It had been a happy day. She was going out with Simon then, and she hadn't even heard of Clett Drummond.

She had to stop thinking of him.

Normally Rowan used her weekends

to plan the week's school activities, but so far she had done nothing. She hated facing the children on a Monday morning with no thought of a structure to the coming week. She'd become so involved with other things that she'd let her responsibilities slip.

She pondered as she walked. The spring, new things growing, baby animals being born — that would be her theme for the week.

New beginnings, a new start. It seemed appropriate, somehow.

Trapped

When Rowan woke up next morning it was to a steel grey day, and the air heavy with the smell of approaching snow. She tapped the long barometer in the hall and frowned at the needle that was registering a temperature drop of ten degrees in the last few days. Shivering, she went back into the kitchen and stood by the window gazing out over the choppy, grey water at the deserted harbour. Wise boat owners, fearful of an approaching storm, had hauled their vessels to safety.

It was the very spot where Clett had stood. Had that been only two days ago? She tried to push the memory of him and Deena, locked in that kiss, out of her mind, but it kept flashing back like a bad dream.

She looked back out at the dark sky.

If it did snow then at least the children would be happy. She pictured the playground full of snowmen and realised she was smiling.

She had waited until the very last minute before venturing out to welcome the children. Clett was bound to be dropping Charlotte and Poppy off and she certainly didn't want to see him today.

Once she'd got her head round the situation she would be better able to cope with it all.

The children were in the playground now, and she had expected to see the top of the Jeep as it headed back towards the farm, but the vehicle was still parked on the other side of the school wall, and Clett was striding towards her.

Rowan's first instinct was to turn and flee back into the schoolhouse, but she knew she couldn't do that. And besides, he'd already seen her.

So she squared her shoulders and went to meet him.

His green eyes were creased with concern as he looked down at her.

'I was trying to call you all day yesterday, Rowan. Where did you get to? I've been worried.'

She shrugged.

'Things to do. Look, I can't stop now, Clett, I have to get the children inside.'

'I'll call round this evening?'

She nodded, anything to escape from those devouring green eyes. He was coming to tell her about Deena. Why else did he look so earnest?

As she and Helen ushered the children into their warm classroom she saw Clett give her daughters a final wave before turning to leave. She was shaking.

There was a murmur of excitement in the classroom as she walked in, and Helen bent her head in a confiding whisper.

'They all know about those pictures of the otters.' She grinned. 'You're a hero!'

Hands were shooting up all around the classroom.

'Did you have to blacken your face, miss, to catch the otters?' Andrew More began.

He was a nine-year-old who was one of three children taxied into school every day from nearby Craigmore village.

'Did you track them?' another child wanted to know.

'Were you wearing a camouflage jacket, miss, so the otters wouldn't see you in the bushes?'

'Can we see the pictures?'

The questions came thick and fast. Across the room she could see Helen stifling a giggle.

'My mum says you were very brave to go to that pond at night all by yourself, Auntie Rowan,' Josh said.

Rowan raised an eyebrow at her nephew. He and Hannah had agreed to address her as Miss Fairlie in school, so as not to suggest favouritism. Clearly, today this didn't apply!

Charlotte and Poppy seemed unaware

that their father had been involved. They were gazing at her with the same apparent hero-worship as the rest of the class.

She shook her head, laughing. There was no point in playing it down, so she described her night's adventure, leaving Clett out of it.

The children were so engrossed in her story that at first no-one noticed the first flakes of snow, so the sound of Poppy's, 'Yippee! It's snowing!' took the class by surprise. Rowan looked out on to a thin carpet of white already covering the playground.

There was a general scrum to get to the windows to see the falling snow and Rowan had to raise her voice to get her class under control.

'The snow will still be there when playtime comes round,' she assured them. 'In the meantime we have work to do.'

She began handing out the jotters she had spent the best part of the previous night marking.

As the children worked, Rowan's

gaze constantly strayed to the window. The snow was getting heavier now, the delicate flakes had given way to clumps and the wind was picking up. From her desk she could see flurries beginning to build in drifts against the playground wall.

It had been years since the village was last cut off. But since the road along the side of the loch was the only access to and from Balcreggan, this was a distinct possibility.

Rowan knew that the steep twisting road, which as the only access to the school from the village, could also be at risk.

'I don't like the look of this, Helen,' she said quietly. 'I think we should get the children home right now!'

The danger point was Dippy Gorge, the local nickname for the notoriously sharp corner and dip in the road. Six-foot snowdrifts could easily collect here if the conditions were severe enough. If there was a continuous deluge on top of that . . .

Rowan shivered. They could have a real problem if she didn't act quickly.

Dolly's appearance seconds later, her plump cheeks crimson and woolly hat and coat caked in snow, brought a wave of giggles from the class. But her expression was troubled as she bustled across the room and whispered in Rowan's ear.

'Things are getting really bad out there.'

'That's it, then,' Rowan said, lowering her voice. 'We need to get these little ones home. Come on, Dolly, help me to phone round the parents.'

With a nod to Helen to take charge of the class, Rowan and Dolly hurried to the staff room in search of the parents' contact details. Taking a sheet each they began to work down the list.

Some parents, concerned by the worsening conditions, had already started arriving to collect their children. Rowan heaved a sigh of relief when she checked the register and saw that, apart from Charlotte, Poppy, Josh

225

and Hannah, only seven other children remained.

Some were getting anxious, and Helen was doing her best to keep them calm.

'Are we going home so we can play in the snow?' six-year-old Thomas Quigley asked.

'I want to go home now!' little Lucy Ryan wailed, sensing all was not right.

The mood of disquiet was spreading and some of the other children began to sniffle.

Helen knew she must keep them occupied.

'Thomas is right,' she said, soothingly. 'Who wants to be in school when you can be at home in your gardens building a snowman? In fact,' she encouraged, 'let's draw the snowman you are going to make at home.'

That had the desired effect. If she could just keep the children occupied until the rest of the parents turned up there would be no problem.

Back in Rowan's office, she and

Dolly were gradually getting through their lists, but the weather had worsened so badly that some worried parents had already rung in asking what they should do. When her mobile trilled Rowan thought it was another parent.

'Rowan? It's James Morrison here.' James ran the village taxi service and was responsible for transporting some of the children from the outlying villages to and from school. 'Is everybody all right up there?'

'James! Thank heavens! We need to get the children home. Could you pick your little ones up right now?'

'That's why I'm ringing, Rowan. The road's blocked. The school is cut off!'

She fought down a rising panic.

'What about snow ploughs?'

'No chance. The village is cut off from the main road as well.'

'Couldn't you get a digger or something to unblock the school road?'

'We're working on it,' he assured her. 'But it's snowing so hard now that as soon as we make any headway that hollow in the road just fills up again.'

She struggled to keep her voice steady.

'James, tell the others not to worry. Everybody here is just fine. We'll keep the children entertained until you get through.'

Rowan put down the phone. She could hardly see out of the window now. She was remembering a winter years ago when the school had been cut off for almost two days. It was frightening — but everybody had survived.

Dolly didn't scare easily, but today she was afraid.

'We will be OK, won't we. Rowan?'

'Of course we will.' She squeezed her friend's hand.

'But we could be here for hours, and it's freezing!' Dolly wailed.

'Well, it won't be freezing in the kitchen once you get that stove going. Off you go, Cook!' Rowan shooed, teasing. 'Feed these children!'

With a positive task to concentrate

on, she knew Dolly would put her fears aside.

'Lunch? Heavens, I forgot about that!' Dolly's hand flew to her mouth and she turned, hurrying in the direction of the school kitchen.

'I think the heating has packed in,' Helen whispered when Rowan got back to the classroom.

Some of the little ones had already started crying.

'I'm cold,' Josh complained.

'So are we.' The chorus went round the room.

Rowan's heart went out to them. She knew she could not show Hannah and Josh any special attention — nor Charlotte and Poppy either — but she longed to hug and reassure all of them.

Then she had an idea.

'We could play musical chairs. That would keep us all warm!'

The children looked at each other, not sure at first what to make of this. Musical Chairs was a party game, and this was school! But Rowan had dug out a radio, crossing her fingers she could find an appropriate station. She found one, and she turned up the volume as high as it would go and helped Helen to rearrange their chairs. It didn't take long for everyone to get into the spirit of the game.

She was so focused on keeping her young charges amused that at first she didn't hear the vehicles. But then, over the sound of the music and the shuffling of little feet as the children jostled to find their chairs, Rowan imagined she could hear the drone of a Jeep's engine. Then there was the chug of a tractor and after that the rumble of a larger, more powerful vehicle.

She went to the window, rubbing a clear circle in the glass and peered out. Through the blizzard she could just make out dark shapes moving carefully into the playground.

Her heart leaped. She and Helen ran to the front door, but before they reached it there was a grating noise as it was forced open and a wall of snow collapsed into the school lobby. Behind it staggered the towering shape of a man, vigorously brushing snow from his hair and face.

The two women stared in astonishment.

'Well, ladies,' a familiar voice said. 'Are we going to evacuate these young people or not?'

Rowan could hardly take in what was happening. But at that moment she could have hugged Clett Drummond, who had rounded up all his farmhands and come to their rescue.

'Come on,' he urged. 'Let's get these little ones into the vehicles. We're taking everybody back to Ballinbrae!'

A buzz of excitement rippled around the room as the adults helped the youngsters struggle into coats, scarves and gloves. Clett glanced around the sea of eager little faces, and smiled.

'Two trips should do it,' he decided.

He had taken control, and she wasn't about to argue.

Rowan and Helen helped the first

group of children clamber safely into the vehicles, making sure the younger ones found places beside Clett in the more comfortable Jeep. With half the youngsters, accompanied by Helen, safely on board for the first trip, the strange little convoy laboured through the blizzard. Ballinbrae Farm was only half a mile along the road, but it seemed to take for ever to get there — and even longer to come back for Rowan and the others.

By the time the convoy reappeared in the playground, snow had once again piled high against the school door and Clett struggled to force it open. The evacuation could have been a nightmare, but it wasn't. He had turned the whole thing into a game. Instead of being terrified, the youngsters were having a great adventure.

Clett alerted the village to what was happening as Rowan and Dolly grabbed what food they could from the kitchen and hastily packed the Jeep with books and pencils to keep the children amused.

In high spirits, they sang their way back to the welcoming farmhouse.

'This is very good of you, Clett,' Rowan said.

He flinched.

'You don't really think I would leave children — not to mention my own two — in that great draughty place? I didn't know the road was blocked until I tried to get down to the village myself. I tried ringing you, but your mobile and the school phone were constantly engaged.'

'Dolly and I were ringing round all the parents to collect their children.'

'I realised that — eventually,' Clett said, turning to look at her. 'It took a bit of time to get the vehicles and drivers rounded up, but we got there.'

'I'm very glad that you did. We could have been cut off back there all day.'

She looked up at him and he gave her a slow, appraising smile that sent her cheeks burning. She looked quickly away. What was she doing, letting this man manipulate her feelings like this? In the turmoil of the last hour she'd forgotten about her misery at seeing Clett and Deena in each other's arms.

Now she wondered what was waiting for them when they arrived at Ballinbrae. Would Deena be there, fussing over the children, casting secret, private smiles in Clett's direction?

She suddenly wanted to throw the vehicle's door open and to jump out into the snow — she wanted to run as far away from this man as she could get. But this wasn't about her. For now, at least, she would have to forget her own feelings and concentrate on looking after the children.

Rowan had been so busy putting her thoughts behind her and helping Helen attend to the children that she hadn't paid much attention to the room. She'd been in it several times since she'd first met Clett. She wasn't even going to think about the last time she saw him in this very place with his beautiful sister-in-law.

But now that she took time to look around properly she realised that more than the walls and the paintings had changed. In the old days, Jack and Sarah Fleming, the elderly couple who worked the farm, cared more for comfort than style. Having no children of their own, they welcomed visits from the village youngsters. The place had been a bit shambling in those days, but homely enough. She remembered two battered old sofas, a couple of oak carver chairs with lumpy cushions, and two black and white collies stretched out in front of the fire.

It didn't look like that now. The granite walls, with their warm cream paint, looked more welcoming than before, and the old oak floor had been restored and was strewn with soft rugs. Brass wall lights cast a cosy glow.

Above the fireplace hung a large painting in soft pastels depicting two children and a woman playing in the sand on an otherwise deserted beach. Their clothes suggested an earlier age.

'It's St Ives.' Clett came to stand beside her. 'We used to take the girls to

Cornwall every year. It's a glorious place.'

Rowan glanced up at him. He was still looking at the painting, remembering those holidays, no doubt.

'I bought it because the children reminded me of Charlotte and Poppy.'

A tug at Rowan's skirt ended the conversation. It was Hannah.

'I'm hungry, Auntie Rowan,' she complained. 'And so is Josh.'

Poppy jumped up from the low table where she'd been busy with other classmates drawing snowy pictures and danced around her father.

'They can have lunch with us, Daddy, can't they?' she pleaded.

'I should hope so.' Dolly Meikle appeared at the sitting-room door, her plump cheeks glowing from the heat of the kitchen. 'Otherwise Mrs Moncrief and I have been working away through there for nothing!'

She caught Clett's eye, seeking his approval to serve the meal they had prepared. On his nod she crooked a finger at the children who followed Dolly's sturdy figure into the kitchen, where a huge pot of broth was simmering on the vast kitchen range, filling the room with its appetizing aroma.

Three plates, heaped with freshly baked cheese scones, had been placed down the centre of the long scrubbed pine table along with two pitchers of milk.

Dolly and Annie had set out bowls of soup earlier and they were now cool enough to spoon up.

Hannah spotted a tray of gingerbread cooling by the stove.

'Yummy!' She beamed. 'When can we start?'

Annie's eyes checked the table.

'We can get most of the little ones around this. The older ones can sit at he small trestle,' she decided.

Rowan hugged the women.

'You're amazing!' she told them warmly.

While the children tucked in to the

meal, she took Annie aside.

'I don't see Miss Traquair here. Surely she hasn't gone outside in this weather?'

'She's gone back to Glasgow. Left first thing this morning, before the snow came.'

Rowan's mind was juggling the possibilities thrown up by this information. Why would she leave so suddenly?

'I thought she was staying on for a while to help with the girls?' Rowan said, struggling to keep her voice casual.

Annie shrugged as her eyes scanned the table, checking if scones or milk needed replenishing.

'I've no idea,' she said distractedly. 'She just up and left.'

Rowan turned away, thoughtful. There had to be a reason for Deena's sudden departure. Then a thought struck her, sending a chill through her whole body. Of course, it was obvious. If Clett had proposed, Deena would have to go back to Glasgow to settle her business affairs. By all accounts she had a high profile job in a promotions company. She would have to give fair notice that she was leaving.

Rowan was certain now that this was the case. She turned to where the children were enjoying their lunch and summoned up all her willpower to force thoughts of Deena and Clett from her mind. She was still responsible for the welfare of all these little ones, and right now that was what mattered most. Her own selfish feelings could wait.

As the children ate, their excited chatter filling the kitchen, none of them noticed it had stopped snowing some time ago. But they all heard a loud thump on the front door.

'They've got through!' Clett called, striding across the flagstones to admit a procession of anxious parents.

Cries of relief filled the farmhouse as they rushed forward to scoop their offspring up into their arms.

Hannah and Josh squealed with delight when they spotted their mother and were scooped up into her arms, a scene that was replicated all over the room as youngsters became reunited with their mums and dads.

The buzz of happy voices was everywhere. Rowan, Helen and Dolly were thanked over and over again for their part in the children's rescue.

'We were all quite safe, you know.' Rowan protested, catching Clett's eye and smiling. 'Mr Drummond saw to that.'

He shook his head to sweep aside the compliment, but Rowan suspected he was pleased at her praise.

It took Clett by surprise when the others crowded round to heap their praises and pump his hand. His voice, when he insisted that any of them would have done the same, seemed suspiciously gruff.

Rowan enjoyed his unease. Balcreggan had made him a hero, and he would have to get used it!

A Guilty Man

Helen left with the last of the children as they were shepherded away by their parents, and Rowan went to give Dolly and Annie a hand clearing up in the kitchen. But they shooed her out, insisting they could manage.

Reluctantly she returned to the sitting-room, where Clett was standing by the fire. Charlotte and Poppy were sprawled at his feet on the carpet, reading.

They all looked up as she came in. Before any of them had a chance to speak she said, 'I have to go, too.'

Clett indicated towards the window where the snow was as deep as ever.

'You can't go back in this. And you certainly can't stay all by yourself in the schoolhouse.'

'Can Miss Fairlie stay here with us, Daddy?' Charlotte closed her book, her expression concerned.

'Yes, please stay, Miss Fairlie.' Poppy had scrambled up and was at her side.

'Of course she's staying.' Clett's voice suggested the matter was settled.

Rowan sighed. Under different circumstances she would have been thrilled to be under the same roof as this man. But if he was going to marry someone else then it would be hard if she stayed.

'My mother will be expecting me down at the cottage. But if you could possibly give me a lift to the schoolhouse to collect a few overnight things then I would be most grateful.'

They all stared at her. She felt bad when she saw the disappointment on the girls' faces. She couldn't fathom Clett's expression. To cover her embarrassment she turned to Charlotte and Poppy and forced a smile.

'At least you two will have a day off school tomorrow.' She glanced out at the white fields. 'You can build that snowman!'

'Will you help us, Miss Fairlie?' Poppy urged.

'I'm sure Miss Fairlie will have other things to do,' her father said sharply.

Rowan didn't have anything else planned, and the girls were making her feel guilty. She was only thinking of herself, wallowing in her own feelings of jealousy. Clett had every right to marry whoever he chose — it had nothing to do with her. Any connection she felt between them had all been in her own imagination.

She squared her shoulders and spoke without a glance in Clett's direction.

'I'd love to help you make a snowman, and if it's OK with your father I'll come back nice and early in the morning.'

The sisters bounced around her in excitement.

'Of course, we'll need a few things to make him.' She put a finger to her lips as though she was considering this. 'We need a nose.'

'Mrs Moncrief will give us a big carrot

from the kitchen!' Poppy squealed.

'Then I can fetch my old red scarf, and we can have buttons for his coat . . . and a hat.' Charlotte turned to Clett. 'Daddy, we need a hat!'

Clett was staring at Rowan, baffled.

'Well? Do you have a hat that would be smart enough for our snowman?'

Rowan found she was grinning at him, and his slow responding smile made her heart thud.

'This sounds like a plan,' he replied, and his green eyes were twinkling.

The journey to her mother's cottage would normally have taken no more than ten minutes, but in the snowy conditions their progress was slow and Clett needed all his concentration just to keep the vehicle on the road.

It didn't stop his occasional sideways glances in Rowan's direction. When he pulled up at Evelyn's gate, he turned to her.

'Is everything all right, Rowan?' He nodded towards Ballinbrae. 'I thought, back there, that something was wrong.'

She forced a smile.

'It's been a traumatic day. I suppose I'm just tired.'

She hadn't intended to mention Deena — his relationship with his sister-in-law was none of her business — but the words were out before she could stop them.

'Annie said Deena went back to Glasgow today. The girls will miss her, even if it's only for a few weeks.'

Clett frowned.

'A few weeks? I think it will be a lot longer than that before Deena will be back in Ballinbrae.'

She raised an eyebrow. A funny tingle started in her toes and worked its way through the rest of her.

'Deena's not coming back?'

He shook his head.

'I shouldn't think so. We didn't part on the best of terms.'

The tingle was becoming a surge and Rowan felt she was in danger of being swept away by it.

'I may as well tell you.' He gave a

little cough, clearing his throat. 'There was a misunderstanding. Don't get me wrong — Deena is a lovely woman, and any man would be proud to have her as his wife. But I'm not that man.'

In the light from the cottage windows she could see his eyes studying her. He was waiting for a response, but she didn't trust herself to speak, so he carried on.

'I'd no idea she was harbouring any thoughts of taking Rachel's place, but apparently that was her plan.'

Rowan found her voice. She still remembered the scene she had walked in on that day. She had to ask.

'And you offered her no encouragement?'

'Quite the opposite. I shouldn't tell you this, but I don't like secrets and I think you should know about it.' He turned away, staring out across the dark harbour. 'There was an embarrassing scene when she tried to . . . that is, she thought I wanted her to kiss me. She threw her arms around my neck

246

and — ' He stopped, shaking his head. 'I won't go into details. Deena was probably as embarrassed as I was.'

Rowan was replaying the scene in her head, the reel scrolling on at a breakneck speed. She could see Deena, her back to the door, her arms around Clett's neck. Had he been trying to keep her at a distance? Was it possible Rowan had totally misjudged the situation?

She couldn't leave it alone.

'I understand that you might not love Deena, but not all marriages are based on love, Clett. Some work very well also on companionship.'

Clett shook his head.

'I'm done with loveless marriages. When I marry again it will be because I am head over heels and hopelessly in love.'

His eyes were searching her face and she had to swallow hard before going on.

'What about the girls?' she asked. 'They think a lot of Deena.'

'They think a lot of you, too, Rowan,' he said, his voice barely more than a whisper.

Somewhere inside her a tiny chink of joy was beginning to grow. It exploded into a starburst when he bent close and she felt the cool softness of his mouth on hers. It was the gentlest of kisses but it sent her heart singing.

He touched her cheek with his fingers, tracing the line of her jaw.

'I'll come back for you in the morning,' he said.

Rowan watched the tail lights of his vehicle disappear back up the hill towards Ballinbrae, and she hugged herself as she opened the door of her mother's cottage and went inside.

★   ★   ★

Despite the excitement of the previous day, Rowan needed no alarm to wake her next morning. From the window of her mother's tiny spare room she could see the sun glinting on the icy waters of a sparkling firth. The hills beyond were glistening white, and when she stretched her neck to peer up the road she could see the snow was as deep as ever.

'Any plans for the day?' Evelyn asked as she added a tomato and a well-cooked sausage to each of their plates of scrambled egg.

She'd been watching her daughter ever since she came in last night, and suspected that it wasn't just the cold that was making her face glow and her eyes sparkle like that.

Rowan nodded, her mouth full of toast.

'Apparently I have a snowman to build.'

Evelyn's eyebrow went up.

'For Hannah and Josh?'

'Um, no, actually.'

Evelyn saw a blush of colour creep into Rowan's cheeks.

'I promised the little Drummond girls I would help them.' She glanced at the clock by the cooker. 'Their father's collecting me in an hour.'

'Is he, now?' Evelyn smiled. 'That'll be nice, dear.'

Rowan ignored her mother's amusement and asked if she'd heard any recent weather forecasts.

'There's no more snow coming today, if that's what you're asking.' She frowned. 'But there's no forecast yet for the rest of the week.'

'That means the school will have to stay closed, for the day at least,' Rowan decided.

The Easter Holidays were only four days away and Rowan was beginning to wonder if the school would open at all before then.

'I'll have to ring round all the parents to let them know what's happening.'

'Two of us doing that job will get through it much quicker,' Evelyn announced. 'So finish up your breakfast and we'll get started.'

All of the parents they called said they had assumed the school would be closed, but everybody thanked mother and daughter for getting in touch. So it was with a clear conscience that Rowan watched for Clett's big car crunching down the hill.

She was out of the gate almost before it came to a halt. Clett got out and came round to open the door for her then turned to wave to Evelyn, who was smiling from the window.

Charlotte and Poppy, dressed in boots, thick jackets, woolly hats and gloves, were running back and forwards in an excited dance outside the farmhouse door when they drove into the yard. Each was waving a plastic carrier bag which, Rowan guessed, contained the vital carrot nose, scarf, hat and buttons.

She laughed and gave them a wave.

'You two look very organised!' she called.

The girls nodded, waiting for the car's engine to stop before rushing forward to greet them.

Clett put up a hand.

'One at a time. Let Rowan get out of

the car before you swamp her.'

But Rowan waved him aside.

'No, they're fine. They just want to get on with it.' She sent Clett a mischievous grin. 'And so do I.'

'Let's do it, then.' He strode towards the vegetable garden at the back of the farmhouse.

Watched by a smiling Annie Moncrief, the four of them rolled snow into a huge ball and began to fashion their snowman. It took half an hour of strenuous effort on the part of all of them before they had anything resembling the character they wanted.

Finally, they all stood back and surveyed their efforts, well satisfied with the results. Clett fetched the carrier bags.

'He just needs the finishing touches.' He handed his daughters a bag each.

Carefully the girls dressed their snowman. Then Rowan stood back to inspect him.

'He looks wonderful!' she said. 'What shall we call him?'

'Mr Frosty!' Poppy squealed.

Clett folded his arms and watched his daughters as they danced around the snowman. He looked up when he saw Rowan watching him, and smiled.

She thought she'd never seen him look so happy. Her mind flew back to only a few short weeks ago when those same green eyes had appeared perpetually troubled. She'd assumed he'd been still grieving for Rachel, but she knew now it had been a loveless marriage, and that Clett's sadness had been for his unhappy little daughters.

They had come to Balcreggan to find a new, happier life. Had they succeeded?

Rowan watched as he chased Charlotte and Poppy round the garden, all three of them now as white as Mr Frosty himself. She saw them collapse laughing in a heap, their bodies making deep imprints in the snow.

Yes, she thought happily. They had succeeded.

A chicken casserole with brown rice

awaited them back in the farmhouse kitchen, and all four tucked ravenously into it. After lunch the girls disappeared into the room Rowan remembered had once been an unused dining-room. Clett had converted it into a playroom for his daughters.

He and Rowan sat on the sofa together, watching the flames dance in the log fire. Then he turned to her, his eyes teasing.

'Your plan worked, then.'

'What plan?'

'The otters. I understand you're now a hero in the eyes of your pupils, Miss Fairlie,' he said, solemnly.

'That was quite embarrassing, actually. I couldn't tell them we were both there that night, could I?' She looked at him from under her lowered eyelashes, teasing. 'We would have scandalised the village!'

But Clett's expression was serious.

'I think we can leave the scandal to Simon Fraser.'

Rowan sighed.

'Oh, Clett. This again? I explained to Simon about the otters and showed him the pictures. He admitted he was in the wrong to accuse Sam, and immediately offered to apologise, which I believe he now has.'

She frowned into the flames, suddenly realising that that had been the last time she'd heard from Simon. It wasn't like him to stay out of touch for more than a day — especially when he must know about the forced evacuation of the school.

'It's odd that he hasn't been in touch,' she said aloud.

Clett got up and went to a tray of drinks he kept on a table behind the sofa.

'Will you join me in a small brandy?'

She nodded and he came back with two balloon-shaped crystal glasses, each containing a measure of the golden liquid. He handed her a glass and sat beside her, gazing into his own goblet.

'The reason you haven't heard from him is . . . he's gone.'

Rowan turned to stare at him.

'What do you mean, gone?'

'Gone. As in vanished. Neither he nor his mother is living at Balcreggan House any more.'

Rowan was stunned.

'But I spoke to both of them there only on Sunday. I don't understand.'

'They've packed their bags and gone,' he persisted. 'But not before leaving instructions with his agent in Inverness to sell the house and estate.'

'Sell Balcreggan? I don't believe it!'

Rowan put a hand to her temple as something further occurred to her. If the estate were to be sold, then Ballinbrae would go with it. What would become of Clett and the girls?

He seemed to read her thoughts.

'I can see what you're thinking, and you're right. We won't be leasing the farm any more. Sam and Dolly will be taking it over.'

Rowan's mouth fell open.

'But don't mention it. They don't know about it yet.'

'You'll be taking the girls back to Glasgow, then?'

Her heart suddenly felt like a lead weight.

'Well, we will be moving from here,' Clett replied, and his eyes had a confusing twinkle. 'But not to Glasgow.'

He was watching her, waiting to study her reaction.

'We're moving to the Big House.'

He caught her hands, forcing her to look at him.

'I've bought Balcreggan Estate.'

Rowan swallowed. She could hardly believe what she was hearing.

Then she remembered the business he had sold in Glasgow. He'd told her it was an engineering company, but he never said the sale would raise enough for the family to afford Balcreggan!

'So what about Simon? I still don't understand why he left, and so suddenly.'

Clett turned back to stare into the fire and Rowan saw his jaw tighten.

'Remember I told you that Rachel

hadn't been alone in the car that night?'

Rowan nodded.

'That other person was Simon Fraser.' He paused. The crackle of the fire cut through the silence.

He went on.

'They'd been having an affair. He confirmed that when I went to see him on Sunday. I must have got there soon after you left, Rowan.

'He wasn't pleased to see me, but this time he couldn't turn me away.'

Clett pulled a brown leather wallet from his pocket and placed it on the sofa between them.

'What is it?'

'The police found this in the car and passed it on to me. They thought it was mine. I didn't recognise it at first, but on Friday night I saw one just like it, when Simon took out his wallet to buy a drink.

'Suddenly it all fell into place. That night, when we came back from the pond, I lay awake for hours working out what to do. I knew I had to confront him, so I went to see him on Sunday and told him what I knew. The evidence wasn't strong enough for the police to make a case of it, but Simon Fraser didn't know that.

'He panicked, thinking no doubt he was about to be arrested for leaving the scene of an accident, maybe that he was even going to be charged with causing a death by dangerous driving.'

Clett gave a humourless smile.

'I hadn't gone to the police with my suspicions, but I didn't tell him that. I got a kind of pleasure out of watching him squirm. I think I wanted to cause him as much pain as he caused my daughters.'

Rowan put her head in her hands. She couldn't take it all in.

'But you have to report your suspicions to the police, Clett. I mean, if Simon was responsible for Rachel's accident that night . . . '

His brow knotted.

'I will. I don't know for sure that he was responsible. It will be in the hands of the law from now on. But when I last saw Simon Fraser he was acting like a very guilty man. He couldn't get out of Balcreggan fast enough. It was handy that he left instructions with his agent in Inverness to put Balcreggan on the market.'

'How did you hear about it so quickly?'

' 'It so happens that Gerry Ballantine, who manages my Inverness business, is friendly with Fraser's man. He mentioned it. Gerry knew I was interested in buying the estate, and that I'd only settled for leasing Ballinbrae in the meantime. He got straight on to me, and the deal was done first thing on Monday.'

Until now Rowan had forgotten about her brandy. Now she swirled it round her glass and took one mighty gulp, spluttering.

'I take it the girls don't yet know any of this?'

Clett shook his head.

'That part involving their mother,

they will never know. But I plan to tell them about Balcreggan tonight after supper.'

He relieved Rowan of her glass and took both her hands in his.

'I was hoping we could tell them together.'

'Clett, this is family business. I'm not sure I should even be there. And you ought to remember Charlotte and Poppy might not even like the place. Balcreggan House is a very big place for three people.'

'Four.' Clett was still watching her. 'Mrs Moncrief will be coming with us.'

'Of course.' Rowan nodded.

'I was hoping for five,' he went on quietly.

'Five?' Rowan repeated weakly.

'I was hoping you would join us, Rowan.' His eyes were gazing at her with such seriousness that her legs were turning to jelly.

'I'm not a housekeeper.'

'I was thinking more along the lines of a wife.'

They stared at each other, neither one daring to move.

'Are you asking me to marry you, Clett?'

He nodded, lifting her fingers to his lips to kiss them.

'That's exactly what I'm doing. I adore you, Rowan. You must know that. We all adore you!'

The tears were stinging her eyes.

'You want to marry me?' she repeated.

He held her close, nuzzling his mouth against her hair.

'You don't have to answer now, my darling. I know I've sprung this on you. All I can wish is that you think about it.'

'I have.' She laughed. 'I've thought about it often!' Then she hesitated. 'If Charlotte and Poppy approve, the answer is yes.'

Rowan had no idea how long the kiss lasted. She only knew she never wanted it to end.

And now it didn't have to. The man

262

she loved had asked her to marry him — and she had agreed.

Clett took her hand, kissing the inside of her wrist.

'I've an idea,' he said, his green eyes full of love. 'Let's not wait until after supper to tell the girls.'

He pulled her gently to her feet.

'What do you say?'

She smiled back.

'I say, let's go and tell them now.'

THE END

We do hope that you have enjoyed reading this large print book.

Did you know that all of our titles are available for purchase?

We publish a wide range of high quality large print books including:
Romances, Mysteries, Classics
General Fiction
Non Fiction and Westerns

Special interest titles available in large print are:
The Little Oxford Dictionary
Music Book, Song Book
Hymn Book, Service Book

Also available from us courtesy of Oxford University Press:
Young Readers' Dictionary
(large print edition)
Young Readers' Thesaurus
(large print edition)

For further information or a free brochure, please contact us at:
Ulverscroft Large Print Books Ltd.,
The Green, Bradgate Road, Anstey,
Leicester, LE7 7FU, England.
Tel: (00 44) 0116 236 4325
Fax: (00 44) 0116 234 0205

A TIME FOR DREAMS

Dawn Bridge

Claire is a teacher awaiting an Ofsted inspection at her school. She discovers that the chief inspector is her former fiancé, Adam, whom she has not seen for five years. Although Claire is now in a relationship with Martin, she is overcome with guilt when she realises she still has feelings for Adam. Suddenly she has to confront her past and decisions have to be made.

THE HEART SHALL CHOOSE

Wendy Kremer

Roark is charming, but emotionally damaged by his broken marriage. Julia quit a relationship when she found her ex-boyfriend was exploiting her. Whilst Julia still hopes to find real love one day, Roark intends to shut love out of his life altogether. Working in a tour company together, their friendship grows — but can Julia storm the barriers that surround his heart? And can Roark forget the past and move on to a better future, before it's too late?